Beneath the Surface
The Elesin Vollan Story

Beneath the Surface

The Elesin Vollan Story

Second Edition

RS Kee

TATE PUBLISHING
AND ENTERPRISES, LLC

Published by Tate Publishing & Enterprises, LLC
127 E. Trade Center Terrace | Mustang, Oklahoma 73064 USA
1.888.361.9473 | www.tatepublishing.com

Tate Publishing is committed to excellence in the publishing industry. The company reflects the philosophy established by the founders, based on Psalm 68:11,
"The Lord gave the word and great was the company of those who published it."

Published in the United States of America

ISBN: 978-1-63306-723-3
1. Fiction / Gay
2. Fiction / Erotica
14.05.05

Don't Care

Alone in my room thinking of you,
I can't get you out of my mind.
No matter how hard I try,
I realize that I,
Don't really want to,
Don't really hate you,
I don't really care.

Maybe it's the loneliness,
Maybe it's the jealousy,
Maybe it's the confusion,
I don't really care.

Sitting in my room thinking of ways,
To get back at you.
I can have any guy I want,
Anything that I want,
But I don't want them.
I don't really care.

What is it that makes me,
Model others to you?
What did you do to me?
You weren't that attractive,
 Hell! You weren't even that nice.

You cheated!
You lied!
You smoked!
And you drank!
And you know what?
I really do care.

Prologue

"Today on Inside News, our top story involves one of today's hottest international pop star—Elesin Vollan. Known for his flamboyant presence on stage, it is the twenty-two year-old's off stage life that has him once again in the midst of scandal.

New images have hit the Internet showing a young Vollan engaged in various sex acts with two unidentified older men. Vollan's relationship with these men is unknown at this time, but it is certain that these images depict a deplorable act on a child.

The graphic photos were first revealed on Jacobsworld.com, which has had 523,500 hits in two days. Vollan's life before N'Step has been something of a well kept secret...

We will keep you updated with the latest developments as this story unfolds. Keep it here on Inside News for late-breaking celebrity news. Next..."

"Fuck me!" I mumbled as I stood frozen in shock with my eyes focused on what seemed like a hundred big screen televisions broadcasting the most traumatizing time of my life. I thought to myself, *how could this have happened?* My heart was racing and my phone began ringing non-stop. I disregarded all calls but one—my publicist, Janet.

"Hello?"

"Have you seen the news?" she shouted into the receiver.

"Uh, yeah! I'm standing in the fuckin' electronics department of Sears. Every television is tuned to this shit." I was outraged at this new revelation of pictures from my past coming back to haunt me. The idea of having something presented to the public of a life that I had never quite come to terms with was frightening.

"Where did these images come from?"

"I don't know…" I replied, practically out of breath as I began running out of the store in a mad dash, hoping that no one would immediately recognize me. Panic consumed my body as I asked for advice on how to handle the situation. We had to assess the damage this could do to my already-tarnishing image. It was going to be hard to control the images of my abuse from the viewing public and even harder to erase them from the Internet.

The images being shown were unlike those that had appeared before. The snapshots of me in drag kissing men at clubs were never really a secret. I just like to keep my private life and my public life separate. After the initial media frenzy, they were chalked up to being in drunken fun or in the name of entertainment. The PR consultants and other staff members did a great job and had successfully downplayed the whole thing and kept my secret quiet.

The fact that I was a young man living with a boyfriend in L.A. somehow eluded the general public since I was married to the woman who was the mother of my son and who was raising my daughter. People naturally assumed that since she and I weren't living together that we were separated. That is, until my very public, very violent break-up with Richard.

Diane interrupted my thoughts, trying to be a voice of reason. "I don't think anything can be done," she said. "The images...the videos...they're all over the Internet. Please, hun, do you know if there are any more?"

"Yes." I was getting more frazzled with every passing minute, biting my bottom lip nervously and I was beginning to taste blood.

"How do you want to handle the situation? I mean, obviously, you'll need to make a statement."

"I was afraid that you were going to say that." I sighed.

"Those pictures from the past you could just blow off. But, honey, no one can sugarcoat these latest photos flooding the Internet. You may need to just give the people what they want, let them know that you are human and vulnerable just like everyone else," she rambled on as my bodyguard and I searched frantically for an exit. "Elesin, it's time for you to let people in. Let them get to know the real you. The fact that you are openly bi-curious or gay never affected your image, so why should this?"

"Because I'm not sure that I know how to talk about this or would want to. I...I just can't! I mean, I was just twelve when those fucking pictures were taken. How could they? I was just a child!" I hissed as we finally made our way out of the store and into the crowd of fans and paparazzi that suddenly surrounded me once outside. Multiple flashing camera lights blinded me and temporarily disoriented my every sense of direction. "I just want this to go away."

"Well, there's no way around it. The photos are out there and you have no choice but to confront this…this abuse. You'll get more sympathy from the public," she explained. "We can try to work on this together. In the mean time, get home and think about what I've said."

This could not have happened at a worse time. Last year was stressful enough. I had been in trouble with my management team for being late, missing gigs and causing conflict within the group. I was still getting over the whole ordeal with Richard and was still dealing with the ordeal that was still making headlines.

Things for this year were supposed to be better for me. The pseudo charmed life I had struggled to maintain in the public eye was beginning to crumble. Diane was right. I was going to have to force myself to share the most horrific time of my life. Unfortunately, I's have to figure out how to come to terms with the abuse first.

All I could think about was how that fucking tape got leaked. Actually, I already knew the how and the who. The only question on my mind now was how to handle this fucked up situation.

As we drove away from the mass chaos that engulfed us, all the memories of abuse—the torture I had suffered as a child…and the life I tried hard to forget—began to resurface. Thirty minutes later as we arrived at our destination. I made a decision. "I guess it's time to return Oprah's call."

Chapter 1
The Early Years

"Ales calm down! It's only for the summer," mother consoled in her thick French accent. I was hiding in my bed room closet with my sister holding me, biting at my bottom lip when my mother found me.

"Your uncle Sebastian is on his way to pick you up...Stop it! You're acting like a little girl," she continued as she picked me up into her arms. My mother always called me by my middle name, Alesand when I was being difficult or in trouble. However, most of the time she would call me Ales (Alice) when she thought that I was acting like a little girl.

Trembling in my mothers' arms, too young to explain how Uncle Sebastian was hurting me. At almost six-years-old, there was no way to comprehend what was being done to my body. I just knew that it was somehow wrong and I was afraid...

"There, there silly boy," she lulled as she continued, calming me into a light whimper. "My little green eyed boy, just look at that little red nose of yours. You look just like your father when he gets upset," she laughed, escorting me to the den with my sister Dehlia trailing close behind.

I was the product of a failed biracial relationship favoring my Scandinavian father in every aspect--from the bright green eyes and wavy honey blonde hair. The only trace of mother was in temperament and my naturally tanned skin. Even though I had a twin sister; she did not share in my likeness nor did she share in my life experiences. She was mother's favorite with her curly sandy colored hair, caramel skin tone and easygoing demeanor.

By age three, it was no secret that my appearance was the subject of much ridicule. Alexander, my father, the philanthropist, traveled the world giving all his attention and love to everyone and everything; except to his children.

Alexander was a free spirited twenty- two-year old who had no sense of responsibility. He was an athletically built man who did whatever he wanted without a care in the world. His family made the bulk of their wealth from the money market and banking. My mother Nyla, a very beautiful brown skinned Mauritian beauty met my father at Tamarin beach and were immediately attracted to each other but it was short lived.

The secret relationship lasted a few months before ending suddenly. The details of the breakup had never been disclosed but its outcome affected how the family treated me. I suspect that hurt my mother in a way that was unforgivable and unforgettable. The results--an unplanned and unwanted pregnancy of twin babies.

My mothers' parents were outraged that their eldest and most promising eighteen year old daughter's life was ruined by "the devil." Fortunately, her parents felt that disowning their

2

child under those circumstances was not an option, so they sent her away with Alexander in Stanstead, Quebec, Canada to have her babies. Being unmarried and promised to another was disastrous. They only hoped Alexander would be responsible and marry her.

Between the stress of both families' hatred and the rage of an alcoholic, adulterer--creating a stable relationship of any kind was virtually impossible. For my mother, the last straw was with him turning his anger on me and my sister Dehlia. She tried everything in her power to keep him away from us and even moved with her parents who were now residing in Baton Rouge, Louisiana.

With my father's wealth and connections, there was no way that he was going to let her off that easy. My sister and I traveled between various homes and countries for awhile; becoming exposed to various cultures, languages and family members whom we'd never met before. When our grandparents, on my mother's side began to come around more, they avoided me like the plague. They cooed over how cute Dehlia was with her pig tails. Captivated over her beautiful skin tone.

"Oh she is just so adorable. She looks just like you," they would say. I resented my sister so much for that. Even though it was not her fault that everyone would oh and ah over her...her bronze skin, sandy tightly curled hair. I had to admit--I was enthralled by her beauty as well.

Compliments were never shared with me-- well, that is not entirely true. My sister would give me a confidence boost from time to time. Nothing I did was ever good enough for either side of my family. I was rejected and dejected. The only acknowledgment of my existence was while I was being disciplined or criticized.

My father had eventually gotten control of his alcoholism, however, the anger and the abuse remained. Sebastian, my father's older brother was the only one who paid any attention to both me and my sister. He would sometimes become a welcomed buffer between us and my father's rage.

Nyla eventually married her parents' ideal mate, Derrick. Derrick was a widower and had a son named Damon from that marriage. Derrick was a very successful investor in Montreal, Canada and provided my mother with the love and respect that she deserved. Derrick was a great guy but I was never able to trust him or anyone for that matter.

They began to notice that my nightmares and erratic behavior would present after my return from my fathers. Derrick would try to comfort me but it never worked.

"Get back to sleep boy. It's only a dream," he'd say, trying to comfort me in his arms as I struggled against his embrace. "Stop it. Stopping fighting me. I will not hurt you." I would scream bloody murder until my mother entered the room.

"What's all this screaming about? Ales calm down!" Mother would get frustrated by my outburst and hysterical screaming. "Talk to me child. Tell me what's wrong? Please Ales." Unable to calm her frightened child, she gave up. "I can't do this anymore, I just can't. I can't help you if you don't talk to me."

"Don't leave me mommy, stay here with me," I whimpered. Mother would rock me in her arms until I fell asleep, with the light in the closet on.

Mother and Derrick soon had a son of their own and their patience with me and my over the top tantrums wore them thin. They were unable to provide me the attention that I needed with a new baby in the house and felt it best to send me off to stay with my father.

It wasn't long after my stay with my father when he had to go away on a business that he enlisted Sebastian and his long time girlfriend Marta to help in watching over me. Father and Sebastian were very close and would do anything for each other. Father knew that he could trust Sebastian and that he could and would give me the attention that I needed. Sebastian was unable to have children of his own due to an infection that was not treated.

It was soon noticed by my parents and Derrick that Sebastian had a way with children. When I was around him, there was no crying, no tantrums, and no problems. They just never realized that I never acted due to fear, fear of what he could do to me or would do to me for that matter. Once my father returned, he faced the same issues and problems with me that my mother had and grew impatient with me. He and my mother began making arrangements for my uncle to help with my upbringing full time. By age five, my uncle had begun to fill the void of my absentee father.

Sebastian was more than willing to be my

legal guardian. This may have been a way for my parent to give him a son that he could never have as well as providing me a positive male influence. And boy did he ever--influence me.

"Oh that must be your uncle at the door," she announced as the doorbell rang. My body stiffed as we approached the door. Opening the door a man who was eager to get me out of my mother's grasp and eager to get me alone to himself.

"I don't want to go mommy, please don't make me go."

"Hey there fella, how are you?" he asked while scooping me up into his arms, "You ready to go?" I closed my eyes hoping that my mom would be able to read my mind and let me stay.

"I will see you soon. Say goodbye to your brother Dehlia," mother said as they saw me off, watching from the porch as Sebastian and I got into his 1982 BMW. Staring at my mother who was waving good-bye as my uncle drove away. Mother was getting smaller and further away as uncle Sebastian continued driving on...until she was gone. I was helpless as I watch out the window, wishing that she could love me...the way that she loved my sister.

My anxiety level rose as the car accelerated. I could not shake the feeling that the summer with my uncle would be worse than the year before.

"We're here buddy!" Uncle Sebastian announced as we arrived to our destination, pulling into the garage. "Let me help you out." Once in the house, Sebastian asked if I were hungry. Getting no response he proceeded to put my things into my room. After getting settled, he made us some sandwiches.

"We're going to have so much fun together," he smiled. "I've got a lot of plans for us while Marta is away," he said while rubbing my leg.

"Okay," I said. That was all I could say as I stared into my sandwich trying to hold back the tears. Only able to take a couple of bites. My appetite lost just as I was.

"You finished?" Shrugging my shoulders as Uncle Sebastian cleared the table. The life that I had grown accustomed to was no more. Mother had pushed me away more and more each year and I wondered if I would ever get back home. Would she ever accept me?

Later that night, Sebastian came into my room to lie beside me. He began stroking my hair, and then slid his hand down the side of my neck as I lay in a fetal position.

"Don't," I murmured, stopping his roaming hand with mine to keep his from going any farther.

"I won't hurt you," he reassured kissing my cheek and then my shoulder. Rolling me over onto my back. "Be a good little boy for your uncle," he whispered. Touching me and making me do things to him that I did not won't to do. Things I hoped I could easily forget.

When it was over, I laid awake--crying and confused. Finding it impossible to fall asleep. Jumping to every creek, every thud I heard-- wondering if he would come back.

It wasn't long after my arrival that my uncle began lending me out to his friends. Every week, it was someone different. One in particular, Jake, hurt me so bad that night that I stayed in bed for three days after. Barely able to walk, barely able to keep my head up. I hated it here and being used but there was nothing that I could do about.

Sebastian loved having sex parties. The men taking their turn with me as the others looked on. Snapping pictures and making videos to immortalize my nightmare. This was never going to end. I couldn't even seek refuge with Marta who was just as crazy and could find ways to inflict pain onto me for sport.

I had been living with my uncle for two months when he began renting me out to his best friend Jake for the whole week. I had never been so scared in my whole life. Jake was a swarmy looking man who worked with the government as a consultant. He was short, stocky and had balding salt and peppered hair. When we were together, he was always bit too rough for me...to me. I would always have nightmares of the snake wrapped around a dagger tattooed on his forearm. I would focus on his tattoo while he was raping me, wishing that I could somehow take the dagger from his arm and use it to stop him from hurting me.

Jake had purchased my company for another fun filled weekend. He had gotten a bit carried away with me; I did not mean to bite him. He was just hurting me so bad that I had to do something to stop the pain but the more I fought the angrier he got. I tried to comply with everything that he asked of me but...I just couldn't do it. It was too unbearable.

"Elesin, be a good little boy and do what

you are told. It won't hurt you if you don't fight," he'd say.

"Please don't."

"Shhh. This is going to happen no matter how much you cry. Just take it like a good little boy." I screamed out as he entered my body. I trembled in uncontrollable fear and pain that I began to hyperventilate.

In frustration, he beat the shit out of me then worked me over so bad that I laid there unconscious. In a panic, my uncle was called out to figure out what to do about my body. Sebastian solution, was to take me out into the woods and make it appear as if I were abducted, raped--then killed. I was found with a knife sticking out of my chest. I couldn't be sure who assaulted me. All I knew was that in their attempt to kill me, they left me there--in the woods alone...naked.

Soon after that incident, my mother decided to try to care for me. I imagined her actions were more out of pity than love. She still did not know how to treat me after that. She was unable to rationalize how a boy could be raped. The next question on her mind was why I ran away from my uncle, but she never felt the need question Sebastian's story.

My uncle came to visit me check up on me often while I was with my mother. Little did they know that Sebastian was just ensuring that I did not reveal what had really happened to me.

"Remember, this is all going to be our little secret. If you tell your mother what happened, she will not believe you and send you away forever," he said. No one seemed to care or notice that I did not speak for over two months. I was too frightened to say anything, not even to my sister who tried to entertain me unsuccessfully.

My mother was barely able to look at me after my rape. She and Derrick never knew how to help me cope with what had happened to me. I would go to hug her and she would push me away as if I had a contagious disease.

"Mommy?"

"What do you want boy?" She asked with a stern tone that startled me. "Well, speak boy." I felt as if I were in trouble for something. Her stare seemed empty and uncaring. I just stood there, sulking. "Ah, boy. You are too soft. You cry about everything. We need to toughen you up like your brothers." She took my hand and led me outside to Derrick and DJ who were kicking the football around.

"What is wrong with him now?" Derrick asked.

"Who knows? He cries too much. Like a little girl. I don't know what to do with him." Derrick suggested that I hang out with them and he would try to do more things with me. Toughen me up. Derrick had tried to be more of a father figure to me but I kept him at a distance.

My step brother, Damon was also never sympathetic to what had happened to me nor did he have patience for my temperaments. He was four years older than me and just as mean as the men who raped me. He also did not have a problem calling me every derogatory name in the book.

Naturally at six, I did not know what a faggot or queer were but I was called one almost every day that I was home, "Elesin, you are such a cry baby," he'd taunt as he hit me in the arm. My sister would come to my aid and stop Damon and DJ from doing me more harm.

"You boys stop hitting Elesin, you meanies," Dehlia scolded as she took me by the hand and led me away. I cried everyday and could never explain why.

Bedtime was especially hard on me, even as Dehlia tried comforting me by sleeping next to me in my bed. The image of that snake tattoo doing harm to my body was etched into my brain and I was unable to control the gurgled screams that emerged from my throat. I wished that I could explain to my family what I was going through, what my dreams were about but I couldn't.

By age seven, I had been tested for everything from autism to social disorders it was soon discovered that I tested at a genius level and may have been a contributor for my "unusual behavior." The high scores and family money allowed me to be educated at an elite private institution. Both my parents and Derrick felt that it would be best to allow my uncle to raise me full time during the school year. I apparently needed more specialized attention than they were incapable of giving.

My birthdays were typically spent with my uncle. Those times in the three years that I was with him were especially hard on me. Every year, would reflect the number of men my uncle had me entertain. Fun times for them but never for me. From that point on, let's just say--celebrating birthdays were never my thing.

I was disgusted with the things that I had to do and was too afraid to say anything and like a good little boy, I never did. I'd just stay out of the way, tucked away in my room escaping my world by singing and writing poetry. As my uncle would always say, "who would believe you?" He was right. Who would? My uncle was a great man who helped his brother in his time of need by stepping in to raise his messed up son. I had no one to turn too, I was just a kid and one believes anything kids have to say about.

My mother never could accepted the fact that I had been raped years ago. By age ten, I had more stress and had experienced more than anyone my age should have to deal with but I eventually learned to adapt. I learned to do everything I was asked and kept quiet.

I was eventually taken out of the school due to behavioral issues and got to move back full time with my mother. Finally, I was where I needed to be. I was still unhappy but I no longer had the fear of having someone entering my room and wanting-- well me.

Still, it was hard to fit into my mother's life and even harder to reconnect with my sister who had her own life and new friends. Surprisingly, my stepfather had become more patient with me and attempted to fill the void that my father had left. With the summer fast approaching, my stepfather had planned a trip back home to the Republic of

Mauritius to visit family. It was strongly advised that I should stay with my uncle while they were away. I had always known that the color of my skin made my family uncomfortable but it was never verbalized.

"I don't think it would be wise for you to come with us," mother said. "I'm afraid that you would not be welcomed."

"Why not? Dehlia is going. "

"That's different. She's--don't worry about her. You will need to stay with Sebastian for the summer while we are away. "

"But I promise to be good; I'll stay out of the way. Please don't send me away," I begged. It took three days of pleading my case before mother and Derrick agreed to let me go. Finally, I felt as if I was slowly becoming a part of the family. Even if it were temporary. The trip to Mauritius was uneventful but absolutely beautiful. Observing the volcanic island surrounded by mountains, beautifully clear waters and white beaches was amazing.

It was nice to see where we had come from. It was great being back home. We met with cousins, grandparents and others that we had not seen in years. All were fascinated with me and my white skin but treated me no different. Even though the family rarely interacted with me at first, I was able to have the time of my life. I played with not only the kids in the area but cousins as well.

Dehlia and I got to actually bond quite a bit while on vacation. Although my sister and I were never truly close. We could still sense each others' feelings and knew when the other was in trouble. I never knew about the dreams she had about me until we went off to explore the beaches. We managed to find a secluded spot on the beach when she confronted me about her dreams.

"Ales--I have been having these weird dreams about you. Is someone hurting you?"

I was shocked. I didn't know how to respond to her random question. "What do you mean," I asked.

"Well. I'm not sure but is someone hitting you or--"she trailed off. Looking off into the distance she continued, "Is Uncle Sebastian doing things to you? Touching you in the bad place?"

I was so ashamed that I could not even look her in the eyes. I just nodded. Then she asked, "Does it hurt? What he does to you?"

"Yes. Sometimes."

"Do you cry?"

"Not always. I just try to pretend to be somewhere else." We both stared off into space. Avoiding the realness of what was disclosed. Then I quickly added, "Please don't tell anyone."

"I won't." She grabbed my hand and led us away towards the water. We splashed around the water, pretending for the moment that nothing was wrong. This moment made us as close as we would ever get. She would be there support system...Someone I could talk to without judgment and nothing more. After all, she was mother's favorite child.

When Dehlia and I were not together, me and some of the kids in the area frequented the beaches where I learned to surf. We played a lot of volleyball and soccer. Not only did I enjoy the scenery but the impression of family unity…even if I were not always included. This was the best time I had ever had in my life. A summer I would never forget.

Chapter 2
The Betrayal

I had been living with my mother for two years and thankfully only seeing my uncle on rare occasions. Fortunately, I was getting too old for most of his friends. But Jake would not go away. He loved to push the boundaries with me. He was a sadistic bastard with too much free time and money at his disposal. The torturous acts he created were not only for his amusement, but he also liked to watch me suffer unfathomable pain. Most of his "new games" involved electrical currents to various parts of my body.

Once I was back home with my mother, I'd be withdrawn from everything and everyone. It was getting too hard for me to go through the motions of being "normal" after being subjected to such horrific and sexually deviant acts. So I crawled into my emotional shell. Then I had to deal with the spawns of Satan—Damon and DJ.

I could be locked in a room all day and not do or say anything to anyone, but somehow I'd get blamed or punished for everything that went wrong. When mother would ask who did what, the boys would yell, "Elesin!" answering almost in unison, pointing their crooked fingers in my direction. I hated those two so much, but I also wanted desperately to be accepted by them, to be a part of a

16

real family.

When I was twelve, my life changed drastically. I never did fit into my mother's life, nor did I fit into the lives of my brothers. Derrick, my stepfather, was the only one who tried to work with me and establish some sort of relationship with me, but it fell apart. I think I was too resentful of the relationship he had with his own two sons to even bother.

Like any father, Derrick could be very strict at times, but I had never had a problem with him or his rules. He tried being civil with me, yet it was still hard for him to accept me. Because of my complexion and my looks, I was an outcast. Even shopping proved difficult for both my mother and stepfather, seeing the looks on people's faces— the looks of confusion—was awkward. Individuals obviously wondered why I looked the way I did and how I fit into the family.

My stepbrother Damon, who was sixteen, would intentionally provoke me by pushing me around and picking fights. Mother never saw him or DJ start anything with me, but she and Derrick always saw my retaliations.
I may have been smaller than Damon, but I could hold my own. If he pushed me, I'd push back harder. If he hit me, I'd hit him back with everything I had. I wasn't afraid of him. After all, I had fought off bigger.

Despite being a misfit in my own family and despite the abuse, academically I was tested at genius level, and started high school at age twelve. That meant I was forced to go school with the devil himself—Damon. He not only prided himself in making my home life miserable, but he made it virtually impossible for me at school.

If being a social pariah wasn't enough, Damon had the audacity to call me faggot and queer amongst his friends. Then he would say things like I was ashamed of my black mother and felt that I was better than they were. I would get beaten up and bullied almost every day by my brother and his friends. Not a day went by when I didn't get cat called or insulted. It had gotten worse after an incident in the boys' locker room. I was putting away equipment and towels in the gym and I guess I looked at a guy too long. Ever since then, I had become the official school faggot.

Every day I'd heard, "Hey faggot! Wanna suck me off before class?" The boys would taunt me continuously as they pushed me into lockers or down onto the ground. I would walk the halls with my head down in the hopes that the day would pass quickly.

I could almost handle my older brother picking on me, but the fact that he never stopped the other kids from pestering me or beating me up made him more of an asshole. I would get pushed and have my head dunked in toilets and Jell-O dumped in my hair. In fact, Damon would egg them on and join in on my humiliation. Most of the time, I could take it, but then other times, not so much.

I never wanted any of them to see me cry. Unfortunately, I was not always that strong. I would break down in the restrooms, that is, if I could make it. The boys would follow me and continue their verbal assaults and I'd crouch in the corner, crying and shaking uncontrollably. There was no salvation. I just could not catch a break.

Not even at home could I find sanctuary. My mother was quick to turn a blind eye, not wanting to deal with the drama between me and my brothers. Any and all issues she would chalk up to, "boys being boys." No matter how many times I cried or got hurt, I got no sympathy.

"Just suck it up, Ales. You're too soft," she would say. I had hope that one day my own mother would, for once, take my side, but she never did. After several months had come and gone, my parents grew tired of defusing fights between Damon and me that were getting progressively worse. After smashing a glass vase against Damon's head, she and Derrick felt that it would be wise for me to live with Sebastian permanently.

"Why?" I cried. "It's not fair."

"You're acting out and the conflicts you are causing are too much for me to handle," my mother explained.

"But I can't live with him. I promise, mother, I'll do better. I'll be better," I pleaded. I tried desperately to express how much I needed to be with her, and how I would do everything I could to get along with my brothers.

"Okay, one more chance," she warned. "But if you get into anymore trouble, that's it! I can't deal with this anymore."

"You can't send me back there, mother. You just can't."

"Then you know what you have to do. I

cannot have you influencing your brothers and sister. And that's that. I don't want to hear another word," she finished.

I thought to myself, *God, please help me. Help my mother see. Help her to love me.* Locking myself away in my room, I thought of ways to bypass my brothers pestering. I knew that if I could find ways to avoid conflict both at home and at school, I'd be okay.

It had been a while since my mother talked of sending me away. Things were going well at home and at school. I kept my feelings bottled inside, never lashing out. Unfortunately, that was all about to change. One day Damon invited me to hang out with him and his friends. That was a first. I didn't trust him, but I wanted so much to be a part of his life and to finally be treated with respect, so I went along.

We ditched class and hung out to smoke behind the football field. I was a bit suspicious at first, and then they all made me feel like a part of the gang as we shared stories and jokes. We talked about things we wanted to do and places we wanted to go. It was a fun time. Then it all changed as fast as the autumn breeze.

Greg, one of the star football players approached me first. "So, I hear that you have a special talent."

"What special talent? What're you talking about?"

"We heard that you were really good at sucking cock." My eyes widened. I was mortified. I began to slowly back away. "Get down on your knees, faggot! You're going to give us all blow jobs," he commanded.

Frozen in fear, my jaw dropped. "What?" I exhaled looked around nervously for a way out, an escape. Trying to process what was happening, I turned to see my brother who was walking away, leaving me alone with his friends.

"Damon!" I yelled. He never turned back. He held his hand up and waved me off as his friends Mark and Greg, who both looked like they had been cut out an Abercrombie and Fitch ad, stepped slowly toward me. They began encircling me and I felt trapped. I took a deep breath and closed my eyes. Then I fell to my knees, doing everything they asked. The whole time I thought to myself, *Lord, just don't let anyone find out. Don't let my mother find out.*

Just as I was finishing off Brian, a voice from across the field called out to us.

"Hey! What the hell is going on there?" It was one of the coaches. He was running toward us in a mad dash. In a panic, the boys quickly straightened up their clothing. I remained on my knees, unable to move.

"Get up, kid!" the coach ordered as he got closer to us. "Now!"

I shuddered as the words pierced through my body like a shock wave.

"He offered, sir!" Mark snapped, trying to deflect the blame as he looked to his buddies for support.

"Yeah! He's a fa--"

"I don't want to hear it," coach shouted.

"Disgusting! Disgusting boys! All of you!" Looking at me, the coach directed his next comment to me. "This behavior will not be tolerated at all. Queer or not, this is unacceptable!" He escorted us all to the principal's office.

My mother and stepfather were called and they were livid. As the principal expressed his disappointment, he laid out my options which were expulsion or home schooling. My parents quickly chose home schooling. For my mother, that incident was the last straw. I was being sent to live with my uncle for good and I was to leave that day.

"But it wasn't my fault, mother," I cried. "Please let me stay."

"It's for your own good," she said as she packed my suitcase. "I just don't understand why you would do such a thing," she yelled. "Repulsive child! I can't have you influencing the other children with your...your sickness."

"But mother, please...don't do this to me. Don't send me back to him. He...he hurts me."

"You need to be hurt. We should all beat that sickness out of you," she screamed. "How could you even think to do...Ugh! Where did you learn such a thing?" she hissed in frustration.

"Uncle Sebastian!"

"Uncle Sebastian what?"

"Uncle Sebastian makes me do those things."

"What things?"

"He," I bit my lip nervously. "He rapes me, mother!" I finally blurted.

"Liar!" she snapped, slapping me hard

across the face. "You're a liar! Little boys don't get raped," she gasped. She rushed out of the room in disgust, leaving me alone...again.

I let out a primal scream that rose from the depths of my stomach. I collapsed onto the floor, crying in hysterics, in utter disbelief that my mother still believed that little boys could not be raped. After what happened to me when I was six, her denial was incomprehensible.

As the minutes flew by, the horror of what was to come flooded my mind. My hysterical cries had turned to soft sobs, knowing that soon I would have no safe haven away from my uncle's abuse. I crunched up into the fetal position beside my bed. My only thought was my life, what was left of it, was over.

He's going to kill me for telling, I said to myself.

Just then I heard my sister enter the room. With her high pitched voice, she said, "You're so dramatic. Nothing's going to happen to you, Ales." I was heartbroken. I just shook my head. There was no point in explaining. She, like mother, never believed that I was raped when I was six. I was so upset that I could barely breathe.

I was surprised when Dehlia held me tightly in her arms until I calmed. I was so distraught that neither one of us even noticed that mother had entered to room with Sebastian.

"Dehlia, leave us," she commanded. My sister kissed me on the cheek, rose from beside me and slowly exited the room.

"I can no longer deal with him. He will say

anything to get out of what he's done," she informed Sebastian as he just stared with a gaze that could cut glass.

"So what did he do that you needed me to rush over to get him?" he asked.

I was unable to look at either one of them. I kept my puffy eyes locked on the floor while my mother explained the events that led up to the phone call. She then ended with the accusation I made of Sebastian abusing me.

"Can you believe that? I'm done. I cannot help him," she said while throwing her hands in the air in surrender.

"Wow, that's quite a story you told there, Elesin." Sebastian hovered over me, never once breaking away from his intense stare.

"Look at me. Did I ever rape you like your mother said?" he asked, trying to clear his name from the allegations of abuse.

"No," I mumbled.

"Why would you lie like that to your mother?"

"I'm sorry," I uttered. The words were barely audible to my uncle who was standing right in front of me. I knew I was in for it. Sebastian asked mother to leave us as he disciplined me and she obliged.

"Please don't...I'm sorry I told—" I pleaded as Sebastian began undoing the buckle on his belt. "Don't hurt me." With that, he slapped me across the face so hard that I fell backwards onto the bed.

"You know better than that," he said as he began to turn me around and beat me with his belt buckle across my backside. I screamed in agony as the metal seemed to rip through my flesh.

After the beating, he forced my pants down and mounted me. He thrust himself inside me with such unrestrained hatred that I bit a hole through the pillowcase.

"Just wait until I get you home," he groaned.

Mother walked into the room just as Sebastian was zipping up his pants and I scurried to pull up my pants. Her eyes were wide and I could tell she was confused by what she was witnessing, yet, she said nothing. I knew then, from the look in mother's uncaring eyes, that I didn't matter—that I was no longer her son. It was there, in my room, that a piece of me died.

As Sebastian and I were leaving, no one said a word. Life in the Benet household would continue on without me. Most hurtful of all, my sister did not see me off. My mother met us downstairs with my bags at the door. She didn't even turn to look at me.

"Please, don't do this," I tried again to plead my case, knowing full well that it was pointless. Mother would never see or accept that she was making a mistake.

"Enough!" she snapped. "I don't want to hear it. Just go."

"But I'm your son. Please forgive me," I wailed. "Don't send me away."

"How could I forgive? You…you…you evil boy." My mother stood firm, unwavering in her decision as my brothers snickered in the background, completely amused at my disgrace.

"I told you, mother. I told you he was gay."

Damon chuckled. My feet were planted in place. I replayed the series of events that had just occurred and could not believe it.

"It's not fair," I screamed. "This is so not fair!"

"Life isn't fair. And you better believe that this incident won't be forgotten," Sebastian said with a grimace. He continued speaking with my mother, making plans to become my legal guardian. I was devastated.

Once I was in the car, Damon ran to the door with a smile on his face. He waved me away and shouted, "Bye, sweet pants." I hated him so much. I hated them all.

As we pulled away, Sebastian said, "You almost ruined everything, you little bastard. Just you wait. I've got big plans for you."

Chapter 3
Living Hell

An hour and a half later, we arrived to my hell, the house where all my nightmares began and will never end. The moment the car stopped, I hopped out and darted for the front door, which I knew he never locked. Living in the middle of nowhere, there was no need. I bolted up the stairs, taking them two at a time. When I reached my room, I turned the knob, but it was locked! "Damn it!"

"You think that you can escape your punishment?" he growled, coming up behind me. He slammed me up against the door. I pleaded with him to forgive me and not hurt me. Suddenly, flooded with a wave of debilitating anxiety, I blacked out.

I awakened surrounded by darkness. My hands and feet were bound to a bedpost. My body felt stiff and sore as I wrestled with the ties that etched into my skin. Then I heard a noise. I was not alone.

"Ah, you're awake," Sebastian said, leaning over me. His warm breath felt like it was melting my cheek, as he whispered, "Now I'm gonna show you what happens to little boys who can't keep secrets."

I was so defeated. I couldn't even muster

the energy to cry. My will to fight—gone. Then I heard an echo of light chatter and shuffling feet. We were not alone. My uncle ran his fingers through my hair.

"I hope you don't mind, but I've invited some friends over to have some fun with me. They've certainly missed you." He chuckled as the men had their way with me. One after the other, they took me from behind, raping me, degrading me. I was uncertain how many of them partook in the brutality and honestly, I didn't care. I just wanted it to be over.

My body eventually went numb from the merry-go-round of men pounding into me. All I could do was close my eyes and pray that it would all end soon. Hopefully, the men would tire and end my suffering.

I prayed to God as the men continuously sodomized me. "Please, if you exist, if you can hear me, help me! Just make it stop. Please, make it all stop," I repeated over and over until I could no longer think. My prayers went unanswered as I slipped into unconsciousness.

Waking up, barely able to move, everything on me was sore. My hands and feet were finally free, though. My throat felt dry and scratchy. I tried to rise but couldn't. The pain so great that tears began to stream down the corners of my eyes. I heard Sebastian's haughty voice coming from across the room.

"You ready for more?" He laughed.

Struggling to speak, I begged, "Water...please." The pain in just uttering those two words was excruciating. It was like I had swallowed shattered glass. The things those men did to me, the things my uncle was going to keep doing to me, were all inconceivable.

Sebastian had left and returned to the room with a glass of water. Placing the straw up to my dry, cracked lips, the cool water stung my throat like acid. My windpipe was probably raw from screaming and… the other things.

"You brought this on yourself, you know? All you had to do was keep quiet. Fortunate for you, your mother didn't believe you," he said. "I've got big plans for you." His abuse was going to be easier to hide now that I had to be home schooled. To ensure that there would be no chance of me speaking out again, he enlisted his perverted friends to do the teaching. Over the next few months, I would do five to six hours of school work and in between subjects, I would service my teacher. At night, when my uncle was home, I would service him. That was my routine. It was my life.

My needs no longer mattered. Actually, they never mattered. I was a sex slave. Doing what was expected, without hesitation.

Six months had passed since I was forced from my mother's home and not one person from that house called to check on me, not once. Not even Dehlia.

I was truly living in isolation, just my uncle and his friends. It was amazing how many friends he had. A few, though, did not share in his fondness for boys. One in particular, Richard Shuffer, was our family's financial consultant. I had seen him a couple times before with my dad when they conducted business, but there was something different about him as he started coming around more for social visits. Richard was absolutely gorgeous and caught my eye. He was six feet three inches tall with brown hair and light brown eyes. His skin was beautifully tanned highlighting his perfect mix of German and Iranian features.

I guess I had begun to develop a bit of a crush. Actually, it was more like a strong attraction for the twenty-seven year old man. Since he and my uncle were close friends, I got to see Richard a lot, especially during football games.

It did not take long before Richard began looking at me with a certain gleam in his eyes. It definitely wasn't the same look Sebastian and his buddies showed me. It was nicer, friendlier, almost inviting. We would kick the soccer ball around, play basketball and video games when Sebastian was busy with work. He was so nice to me. I felt like I finally had, well, a friend.

Sometime after my thirteenth birthday, he invited me to go camping with him. Surprisingly, my uncle allowed the outing. The whole trip was amazing. I learned how to fish, make a fire and other survival techniques. On the second night of camping, we decided to do a little skinny dipping. We splashed around in the water, wrestling each other. We were having the time of our lives.

The moon was full. The water was glistening off of his amazing, muscular body and I got excited, too excited, and he noticed. I was so embarrassed that I hurried out of water. He ran up behind me and reassured me that everything was okay.

"Don't be embarrassed, Elesin. It happens," he said. Looking down, I noticed that he had the same reaction. He ran his hand through my wet hair and leaned in and kissed me. It felt so good, so right. The kisses got deeper as he lifted me up and cupped my ass in his hands. I stood on the tips of my toes and used my tongue to trace along his neck. He let out a moan.

He laid me down onto the ground, kissing every inch of my body. For the first time, I made love, under the stars. The feeling was totally different from what I had ever experienced with Sebastian and his friends. That was sex, control, power. With Richard it was love. It felt natural and right. I screamed with pleasure as my body released everything with every thrust of his pelvis.

The anger, the tension, and the fear that normally consumed me were gone. At that moment, I finally felt calm. We lay in each other's arms and held each other tight, loving each other several times that night.

I returned from the camping trip with a smile on my face. The only thing on my mind was Richard. It was hard to focus on anything else. Somehow, I actually managed to concentrate enough on my studies to complete my school credits.

After my time away with Richard, I was consumed with thoughts of leaving Sebastian's evil house of terror. Even if it were only for a few minutes, I needed time to myself, time to be a kid.

Marta, my uncle's girlfriend, who was just

as sadistic as he was, had spoken to my uncle about getting me into a sport or some sort of activity. She took me to Centauri Summer Arts Camp, which offered not only academic courses but artistic programs as well. It was there that I discovered dance and music and with a little coaxing, I was in.

Through dance and music, I was able to be free. I was free to express my frustration and pain without words. Marta supported everything I did. Anything that kept me from home and away from my uncle, she was all for.

That lady was a real head case, but she was the closest thing to a mother figure that I had. I was grateful to her because she would shuttle me to and from my classes. I submerged myself in as many courses as I could. That way, I would not be at home as much with them...with him.

A few weeks into my courses, Sebastian stopped having sex with Marta. They never had a healthy sex life to begin with, especially since Sebastian had a fondness for little boys. One day my uncle was away and Marta decided to use me for her sexual outlet. That was the first time she had sex with me without my uncle being there.

I had never thought of sex with a woman before and was caught off guard by it at first when she approached me. I was on my bed writing when Marta made her move on me. At first she ran her fingers through my hair and leaned into kiss my neck. I looked up to her and smiled thinking that she was just having a tender moment. Then she took my face in her hands and kissed my lips the way that Sebastian did, only her lips were softer.

She began undressing in front of me as lay there confused. "Sebastian can't be the only one to enjoy your company. Now it's time for you to show me the love that I've shown you." I was so scared. "Touch me." She turned me onto my back, straddled me and placed my hands on her breasts. Then she pinned my hands above my head and began to undress me. My eyes were wide with wonderment and I began to shake nervously.

Marta leaned into me, looked me straight into the eyes and said, "I'm going to teach you how to make love to a woman." Sex with Marta was dangerously exciting. I had never felt as empowered as I did when we were together. We had sex all day with Marta teaching me how to please a woman, how to control myself and how to love. I didn't mind doing things with her. It was different.

Richard would stop by to visit me during my breaks from class. I had developed strong feelings for him. It was apparent that he felt the same about me. After a while, Richard began picking me up from class and taking me home. One late afternoon, when he dropped me off, I stepped into the house and it looked like a war zone. Pictures were thrown onto the floor, furniture flipped over and broken glass everywhere.

"Hello?" I shouted as I cautiously followed the trail of devastation. Unaware of my uncle's presence, it was too late. I was knocked to the ground and kicked. I let out a piercing scream, but my uncle continued kicking and stomping on me.

"You little bastard," he hissed. He reached down and slapped me across the face—hard

"You've knocked her up."

"I'm sorry," I apologized, although I was confused as to what he was talking about. "What did I do wrong?" I asked with blood trickling down my lip.

"Marta! You've gotten her pregnant, you little fucker. You've ruined everything."

After the beating, Sebastian stormed out of the room. I remained on the floor for what seemed like an eternity before I managed to rise and finally make it to my room. I collapsed onto my bed, wincing in pain, and cried myself to sleep.

I was awakened by the sound of my room's creaky door. My uncle's heavy footsteps neared my bed.

"Wake up!" he shouted, while snatching the blanket from my bed. "Get downstairs and help Marta in the kitchen." I rose quickly and did as commanded. Consumed my fear, I darted out of the room, avoiding eye contact with my uncle.

"I hate it here," I mumbled on my way to the kitchen. *If only my mother had loved me, none of this would have happened to me. Maybe she's forgiven me and will take me back.*

I assisted Marta with chopping vegetables and prepped for dinner. As I moved about the kitchen, I thought about the new reality. Marta was pregnant. I wondered how this baby could or would change my life. Would I play an important role in its life? Would I be able to love it? Could I be a dad? A parent?

Later that evening, before I went to bed, I called my mother. I was happy that my sister answered.

"Hey, Ales. How are you?"

"Miserable. I miss you so much. I don't want to be here. Do you think that mother will let me come back home?"

"She said that we are not supposed to talk to you. Says you are a bad influence and that you tell horrible lies," she said.

"And you believe her?"

"Um...I don't know. I have never seen Sebastian do anything bad to you. He's disciplined you, but—"

"But you don't believe that he's done anything more?" The long silence said it all. Not even my twin sister believed me. "If I told mother that I lied and that I was sorry, would she let me come back home?"

"Definitely not," she kept her responses hurried and short.

"Are you sure?"

"Yeah, pretty sure. Listen I, uh, I have to go," Dehlia replied quickly to end the call. With nothing more to say, we said our good-byes. It's quite unfortunate that I have absolutely no one to turn to. I don't even have any real friends. If it weren't for Richard, I'd be truly alone.

Over the next couple months, my uncle's abuse, well, the beatings and the late night visits, began to decrease. Guess I was getting too old and too strong for him. At almost fourteen, I was already too old and used up.

But not with Richard, a few months into our secret relationship, I began to confide in him about the terrible things Sebastian was doing to me. I felt that if I told him, he would not betray me as my mother had. I even told him about the baby growing inside Marta. He was so stunned by the revelation he said nothing.

"Would you help me? Help me run away with my child?" I asked.

He laughed uncomfortably. "How am I supposed to do that? I'd be arrested for kidnapping or worse."

"Please." I begged. "Do you love me?"

"Of course, I do. You know I do."

"If you really do love me, you'd do this for me."

Richard took in a deep breath. He kissed me on the forehead and said, "Let me see what I can do." That was all I needed to hear. I knew in my heart that he would come through.

I could easily understand his concern. I was only thirteen years old. No job, a baby on the way and no access to my trust until I turned eighteen. It would be very difficult to pull off, but something had to be done. There was no way I could stand by and see my child go through what I was dealing with. I would rather die than give my child to that monster.

My daughter was born three weeks after my fourteenth birthday. Surprisingly, I was listed as the father on the birth certificate of the beautiful baby girl named Lynnea Rosalie Vollan. She had my green eyes and my curly blonde hair. When I looked at her little face, I knew that I would do anything and everything to protect her. Wow! Holding her for the first time in my arms, the overwhelming love that I felt for her was something I could not comprehend, but I welcomed it.

She looked up into my eyes and I hoped that she'd love me just as much. Looking at her little fingers, her little toes, her little chubby legs, I was amazed. "I helped create this, a whole little person," I ogled. "And she is all mine," I said aloud.

"She sure is and you can have the little bitch," Marta snapped. "Just keep her out of my way and keep her away from Sebastian." Marta stomped off.

It was very clear that Lynnea was not very welcomed in the household. Marta rarely held her or even looked at the baby. If she took care of Lynnea, she would only do so in protest, when Sebastian forced her. So, I had to be Lynnea's mother, her father—her life.

One evening I got a surprise visit from my father. He needed to have some papers signed by Richard. My dad, upon seeing me, had a look of concern on his face, a look I had never seen before.

"Hello, son. How've you been?" he asked as he took me into his arms for a hug.

"Fine, I guess."

"You guess?" He pulled me away to look at me. "What happened to your eye?" He quickly noticed the healing shiner I had
on my left eye. He peered down at me with a suspicious glare, remembering the last time that he made a surprise visit and I had a black eye and busted lip.

"I bumped into the cabinet," I answered unconvincingly.

He shook his head in disbelief. "You need to be more careful. Every time I see you you've got some kind of injury. I just don't believe that you're that clumsy." I did not have time to respond when Sebastian entered the room. My body immediately tensed up at his presence. I had the overwhelming feeling that I was in trouble for something but I had no idea what.

"Alexander, what are you doing here? I had no idea you were in town. What's going on, bro?" Sebastian asked.

"Oh, I just have some papers for you to sign, nothing major. Hey, is everything all right with Elesin? He's acting kind of weird. I don't know, maybe it's just me."

"Ah, he's always like that. Let's go into the den and get those papers signed," Sebastian said nervously as he quickly escorted my dad to the den. My father kept looking over his shoulder at me. I was nervous as I went off to tend to Lynnea, getting her bathed and ready for bed. Once done, my dad made his way upstairs to find me dressing Lynnea.

"Who is this?" he asked with obvious suspicion as to who and where this baby had come from.

"This is Lynnea, my daughter."

"Your daughter! What the hell do you mean your daughter? How? Who's the mother? And why am I just now finding out about this?" I answered his questions as best I could without giving up Marta as the mother. My dad was pacing, clearly pissed off about my teenage fatherhood. The whole thing did not sit well with him but he soon realized that there was nothing he could do about it and took Lynnea into his arms and marveled at her beauty.

"When will I get to see you again?" I asked.

"Not sure, I'm pretty busy and something just came up that I need to take care of. I'll be meeting with Richard to finalize this paperwork," he answered as he rocked Lynnea to sleep. "I'll try to call you when I can." He took me into his arms and held me tight and for once, I felt safe.

"Okay," I said meekly. "I'll see you then." I knew that it would be awhile before I heard from my dad again. He always had a habit of taking off and disappearing for "work" for months at a time. As my dad and I said our good-byes, I placed Lynnea into her bed and walked with him downstairs into the living room where Sebastian was sitting watching television.

"Elesin, I know that something is going on with you right now and I'm sorry that I haven't been there for you like I should, but just know that everything will work out for you," he reassured. He gave me another hug all the while I wondered what he meant by 'everything would work out for me?' "Could you please give me and your uncle some time alone?" I honored his request and went back upstairs.

I overheard my father raising his voice to Sebastian, reprimanding him about something. It almost sounded like they were arguing about me, but I couldn't quite make it out. Whatever they were arguing about, my dad stormed out, slamming the door behind him. I stood there a while trying to absorb the events of the night. Then I got ready for bed.

It wasn't long before Uncle Sebastian began to look at Lynnea in that way—a way that would make one's skin crawl. I knew that look all too well. I hated him for that look and what typically followed after the look.

Approaching me as I fed her, Uncle Sebastian hovered over us.

"I wonder if she has strong jaw muscles like her father." A wave of fear and disgust flooded my body.

"You stay away from her!" I shouted.

"What are you going to do about it?" My heart sank to the pit of my stomach. Running his finger along my lips, he asked, "What are you willing to do for her?"

"Please don't!" *Was this really happening? Was I really negotiating with my uncle over maintaining my baby's purity?* Yes. The smirk on his face revealed the harsh reality. Closing my eyes, I answered, "I won't fight you. Just please, don't touch her." He smiled, then walked away.

I exhaled, looking down at my little girl. "I just made a deal with the devil." Then I swore to Lynnea that I would do absolutely anything to keep her safe.

Later that afternoon, I put her down for her nap and as I left the room, my uncle called for me downstairs. "Elesin! Where are you, boy?" Feeling the hairs rise on the back of my neck, I took a deep breath, and then hesitantly went to him. He was in the living room, nude. I approached cautiously, as if every step were made in a muddy pit. I slowly dropped to my knees.

"No! Not this time." He pulled me up and began undressing me. "I want to see your face when I enter you." Sebastian pushed me onto the sofa and forced his way into me. "You are such a pretty boy." The guilt of what my uncle was doing to me was too much for me to bear. I tried to escape to a peaceful place in my mind. Keeping my eyes closed tight, I wished I could disappear, just vanish into thin air. The more I flinched in agonizing pain, the more excited he became.

"Ah, you like this, don't you?" he groaned. "Tell me how much you like me pounding in your ass. Tell me how good it is."

At that point I was unable to control the tears from streaming down my face. My bottom lip trembled intensely. When he was about to come, he grabbed my neck and choked the shit out of me. I scratched and tried to pull his hands away, but he was just too strong.

At least that time, I didn't black out. I almost wished I had.

Life went on like that for awhile. I was my uncle's personal sex toy. The things that he forced me to do to him and for him—Jesus!

I couldn't live like that anymore. It was just too much for me to handle, especially now that I had Lynnea.

Chapter 4
Life Changer

Lynnea was the love of my life, she was the most beautiful thing that I had ever seen, unfortunately, Uncle Sebastian noticed too.

"I've always wondered what virgin pussy tastes like."

"Don't you ever come near her! Don't you even look at her!" I scolded. "Please..."

"What are you going to do about it?" he sneered.

"Anything." I was aghast. "You know that I'll do anything you ask. Please, just don't touch her."

He walked off with a sly smirk on his face. The look in his eyes chilled me to the bone. I put Lynnea down in her crib, keeping guard over her until she fell asleep. I slowly made my way out of the room, closing the door softly. I turned to find my uncle standing directly behind me.

"You won't fight me, huh?" I was startled by his sudden appearance. Sebastian slammed me against the door. Typically, I could sometimes fight him off, but this time I couldn't. If I did, he would find a way to get what he wanted.

As quickly as he had appeared, he took me down to the floor, ripping at my clothes. He began biting my neck, sending mind-numbing pain throughout my body. Slapping and pulling my hair, he growled with pleasure as he inflicted me with more pain. It took everything I had not to fight back. I knew that if I did, the outcome would be disastrous.

Pulling down my pants and flipping me around, Sebastian shoved his cock into my ass, letting out all of his aggression and frustration on me. He jabbed me in the ribs and slammed my head to the floor. I fought the cries of pain through clenched teeth.

Thoughts swirled throughout my mind with questions of why. Why does he take pleasure in hurting me, his nephew? The next thing I know, he had hooked his arm around my neck, and I nearly passed out from the lack of oxygen as he continued riding me— hard. Once he was done, I continued to lay there on the floor, curled up into a fetal position, whimpering softly. This was only going to get worse.

I dragged myself from the floor and limped to the restroom to collect my thoughts. Splashing cool water onto my face, I struggled to take in deep breaths. I slowly exhaled all the bad shit I was going through. *Things will get better.* I told myself. *The madness has to end soon.*

Every day with my uncle was becoming more and more torturous. The moment I thought it could not possibly get any worse, it did. He was able to devise new and inventive ways to torture me. He did anything to try to break me. I love my sweet girl, but I was barely hanging on and I didn't know how much more I could take. I was so scared.

And I had no one but Richard. *Fuck!*

"Elesin! Get your ass down here, now!" Sebastian ordered. He just wouldn't stop. He wouldn't leave me alone. *God!* As I walked down the stairs to my doom, I could not imagine what my fate would be. I had done everything that he asked of me, but nothing satisfied him.

"Yes, sir?" I answered, walking toward him with a slow shuffle. He was in the kitchen with this look of absolute disdain.

"I think that you need to be punished. You forgot to rake up the leaves today."

"I'll do them now. I'm sorry."

"No, just go down to the basement."

"No, please, I'm doing it now."

"Do what you are told, boy!" he demanded while grabbing me by the arm and forcing me down the stairs. He shoved me so hard that I tumbled down the flight of stairs. Following close behind, he lifted me up and dropped me onto the cot. After tying my hands and feet tightly with some rope, he cut the clothes off my back and proceeded to whip me. The pain stung my flesh. I screamed in agony.

"PLEASE! STOP!"

But the more I screamed the more he struck me. Then he proceeded to force himself inside me over and over and over again. He left me in the basement for what seemed like days, taking pleasure in my suffering, taking pleasure in my shame.

After raping me, he would lean over and say, "You give up yet?" Never waiting for a response, he'd head up the stairs. Marta would come down shortly after with Lynnea in her arms.

"You foolish boy. I don't know what you've done to upset your uncle, but you better make it right," she said. She continued blaming me for everything that was going wrong.

"Please, Marta, would you help me? I'll do anything. I'm so tired."

She did nothing.

After each session with my uncle, she would simply come down with Lynnea to clean my wounds and provide me soup and water. She was not too happy about having to take care of both me and Lynnea.

Three days later, as if by miracle, Marta showed some semblance of compassion. She freed me from my bindings that had left my hands numb. Bound for a week, in the dark dank room with no windows and dim artificial lighting, I could hardly see and thought I was dreaming.

"You mind your uncle and take care of your responsibilities," she said and then left. I'm not sure how long I lay there, but I woke up to stiff muscles and an unbearably bad headache. I managed to climb the stairs and up to my room. I ran a bath and soaked my sore, battered body. The hot water burned my skin like acid. I sank down into the tub, crying...crying so hard that I began hyperventilating.

"I can't do this anymore. I just can't," I sobbed, scratching at my arms to dull the pain in my heart. I dug my nails deeper into my left arm until it bled.

After collecting myself, I decided to end it

for the both of us, end the pain that I was in. End the pain that could come to my sweet girl. I quietly tiptoed into Lynnea's room. Her face glowed with joy. She was so happy to see me. I gently picked her up and took her to my room. I laid her down gently onto my bed and kissed her sweet little face. I grabbed my tear-stained pillow, squeezed it into my hands and pressed it against her face.

"I'm so sorry. Please forgive me, my love." Lynnea has a strong spirit. She fought and kicked for her life. Fighting with strength that I once had, her tiny arms flailed around. "I can't do this!" I cried as I threw the pillow across the room. I picked up my baby girl and held her close to my chest. "I'm so sorry! I'm so very sorry!" I rocked her in my arms, hoping that she could forgive me, hoping that I could forgive myself. Just hoping…

I decided to call my sister. This time my mother answered the line.

"What do you want?" she barked as if I were a telemarketer and not her first born son.

"Can I speak with Dehlia, please?"

"She's busy!" she snapped back. "It would be wise never to call here again."

"But, why?"

"Just leave it alone. Just forget about me and forget about Dehlia." She hung up without another word.

My appearance, though similar to my father's was no reason to have my mother hate me, I was in no way like my father. I could never hurt my mother the way that he had. In my mother's eyes I represented the evil that was in my father. A lifelong punishment for my mother being betrayed and she never let me forget it. Even through everything I'd been through, it was hard for me not to love her.

I had to maintain hope or I would surely go insane. I dialed Richard, but my attempts to contact him were unsuccessful. *Where the hell was he? Did he just use me for his own selfish reasons? No, no that couldn't be it. He's just busy. That's got to be it. He'll help me. I know he will.*

I had nowhere to go and no one to turn to. So I completed all my chores around the house and tried hard to avoid my uncle at all costs. Sadly, that was not the plan my uncle had for me that night. The door to my bedroom flew open.

My eyes widened in fear. "I've been thinking about our little arrangement," he said with a smirk. "I think that I can get you to fight back. It's really no fun when you don't fight," he said as he yanked me out of bed. Everything was happening so fast. I had not even processed that I had been struck.

Trying unsuccessfully to get up, I asked in a haze of confusion, "What? What did I do wrong?" My focus became clearer and I realized then that I was still in my room.

"You ready to play?" He laughed, kicking me in the ribs. I curled into a ball from the pain. He continued to stomp on my side, then my back. "I've got some new toys for us to play with," he teased.

"Please, not now. Just this one night," I pleaded. "Don't hurt me. I will do whatever you ask. Just don't hurt me anymore." My voice became hoarse from the strain from all the crying. My body weakened and my mind went blank.

Sebastian beat me senseless. My limbs wanted to fight back, but I had nothing left.

"Fight!" he shouted as he pounded into my back. "I said fight, you sorry sack of shit!" I was in so much pain, wailing in agony. I hoped that just once someone would hear me and save me. All I could do was lay motionless on the floor, praying to God that it would be over soon and hoping that Sebastian would tire of beating me or at least get bored and leave me alone. He never did. At least that time he didn't rape me. But I was beaten without mercy.

Incapable of moving, I lay there shaking violently all night on the floor.

The next morning I woke up and crawled myself to the bathroom. I used the sink to pull my weak body up. In the mirror, a face stared back at me that I didn't recognize. I gasped at the hideous sight. Tears streamed down my cheeks. Eventually, I managed to find some pain pills in the cabinets. I hoped that they would work quickly.

My heart raced with fear as I limped around throughout the house. The only sounds I heard were of Lynnea playing with her toys in her crib. Thank God we were alone. The phone rang. It was Richard. He wanted to meet with me to discuss what we had talked about before. He could hear the desperation and fatigue my voice.

"I really need you," I cried into the receiver. "I don't know how much more I can take."

"I'll be right over," he said, reassuring me that everything was going to be okay. After we hung up, I made sure that Lynnea was taken care of, that she was fed and changed before Richard came over.

Richard arrived thirty minutes later. He looked so good. I practically jumped into his arms. The pressure of his biceps wrapping around me hurt my bruised back and I let out an "ouch!"

"My God! What did he do to you?" he asked as the tears I fought to suppress welled up in my eyes. He continued holding and swaying with me until I calmed. He kissed my battered face gently.

"Sorry I haven't called, but I've been away on business," he apologized.

"That's okay. You're here now."

"I've missed you so much, Elesin," he smiled as he kissed my forehead. Then he kissed my lips. His full lips were so soft. Taking my face in his hands he said, "I've got some good news."

Apparently, while he was away, he managed to get some travel documents for both me and Lynnea. He was also able to get access to my father's account and release some funds for me. The best news of all was that we would be able to leave within the week. Hearing this, well, I must have cried into his chest for about ten minutes. I bawled at the realization that all the pain, all the suffering, would finally end. I could at last have peace with my daughter.

When Richard left, the only thing I had on my mind was freedom—our freedom. Freedom from a mother who never loved me, freedom from a father who abandoned me, freedom from an uncle who raped me and freedom to live without fear. Everything was going to be fine, just fine.

Four days later, with my uncle at work and Marta God knows where, it was Richard to the rescue with passports in hand for me and my daughter. My documents, of course, were slightly altered. I was no longer a fifteen-year-old boy. I was now nineteen. Guess it would be more conceivable for a man like Richard to travel with a man of almost twenty than it would if he were traveling with an unrelated, under aged boy. I guess if Richard felt that I could pass for nineteen, why not?

I was tall, just under six feet tall, had a child and with all the stress that I had gone through, I had a more aged look. My eyes no longer glimmered with exuberance and innocence like most teenagers. The youthful life in my eyes was gone.

I called home one last time and was elated that Dehlia answered the phone. I informed her of my departure, but she could care less. I could feel her rolling her eyes as we spoke, rushing the conversation as if I were keeping her from something. She had become more and more like mother as time went on, cold and closed off. I just did not understand why I was alienated the way I was, especially by my twin.

"Dehlia, I just wanted to let you know that I am leaving with Richard today."

"Oh, where will you be headed?"

"His place, I guess. For now, anyway, I just have to get out of here and away from Sebastian. I can't bear to stay here another minute," I explained. The butterflies in the pit of my stomach were fluttering out of control and making me more anxious to leave.

"Ales," she paused. "Did...did he really hurt you? Rape you like you said?"

"If I said yes, would you believe me?"

"I'm so sorry that I never believed you." The sincerity in her voice brought tears to my eyes. She ended by saying, "Elesin, you be safe and call me when you get to wherever you end up." It was really great hearing her voice again. Maybe we would be able to get together one day in the next life, when things were settled.

Before we could travel, I had to heal the wounds I had acquired from Sebastian's latest assault. My uncle had worked me over so bad that five days later, I still walked with a slight limp. I looked too battered and weak to travel and would certainly raise suspicion. I just knew that Sebastian was going to put up a fight to keep me from leaving but the stars were aligned in my favor with my uncle away on an extended business venture.

In the meantime, Lynnea and I stayed with Richard in Stanstead. His small townhouse was cozy and bright.

"How are you feeling today, baby?" Richard asked as I lay in bed.

"I'm okay, I guess," I answered as he lay on top of me, kissing my neck as I held onto him, not wanting to let him go. I had been laying there thinking about how horrible my life had been and wondering if running away with Richard was the best idea.

He must have read my mind. "I'll take care of you from now on. You will have nothing to worry about," he whispered in my ear. I closed my eyes, believing that all would be right with Richard. Life would be good. I deserved it. Hell, Lynnea and I both needed a fresh start.

Chapter 5
Liberation

I had been at Richard's for over two weeks. No one seemed to care that Lynnea and I were missing. Every day, my anxiety levels grew with anticipation that Sebastian would come and take us back. Even though Richard reassured me that I no longer had to worry about Sebastian any more—I did anyway.

While sitting with Lynnea on my lap, a commercial for Mexican travel came across the television screen. It looked so beautiful and peaceful. Cancun...*I sure wouldn't mind going there,* I thought. I imagined getting some sun, having some fun and enjoying life on the beach. I mentioned Cancun to Richard and that I'd love to go there and he did not have any problems with the idea. He said it would be a well-deserved vacation.

Four days later, we were off. We stayed in a secluded but popular location for those who had money to spend. Richard had managed to rent a house at Casa Bella, which was right off the beach and surrounded by the Caribbean Sea. He obviously had expensive tastes. The house also kept with Richard's ideal look; it too was white. The Italian style beachfront villa was surrounded by palm trees with a private pool on the Caribbean.

Traveling across the border was quite easy;

however, the drive to the house was tricky. I don't think that anyone in Mexico really learned how to drive or believed in obeying traffic laws. It was more or less an every-man-for-himself situation.

Once we managed to arrive at our destination in one piece, I got Lynnea fed, changed and off to bed for a nap. It had been an especially long day for her. She was cranky and crying a lot, but once she was comfortable with her surroundings, it was lights out.

Going out onto the patio, I stood, staring at the beach. The beautiful crystal blue and green water was amazing. Richard crept up behind me, holding me tight and kissing the side of my neck.

"I love you," he whispered into my ear. I closed my eyes. My body shivered at his declaration of love.

"I love you too." Taking in the moment, I realized that this was the first time I was at peace. The first time I felt safe. The first time I felt loved.

"How would you like to make this your home, our home?" Richard asked.
Home. That word took on a new meaning to me. Home was no longer threatening; it was now comfortable to me. It felt right, especially when Richard said it.

"I'd love to stay here," I answered.

"I'd still have to travel back home every once and awhile and conduct business, but you could stay here full time. Well, that is, until you get bored with this place," he added.

"That would be great." I turned to face Richard. He took my face into his hands and leaned in to give me the deepest, most passionate kiss he had ever given me. He then hoisted me up and carried me onto the sofa where we made love. It was magical.

Afterward, my nervous energy got the best of me. I was absolutely no help to Richard as he began to prepare dinner for us, laying out the food items along the counter top. Not only was a stranger to Mexico but I even more of a stranger around the kitchen. While Richard continued to make sense of the piles of ingredients being thrown together, I decided to take a walk along the beach to check out the neighborhood. I had walked around for awhile and found a bench next to a taqueria. I stretched my arms wide, resting them on the top of the bench as I enjoyed the view and some alone time. Then I saw him. A six feet tall, gorgeous Latin man walked along the beach and headed in my direction. He glanced over at me and smiled.

Nice!

"Hola!" the handsome man greeted and smiled. "Como esta?" he asked in his native tongue.

I smiled and responded back in Spanish. "Muy bien."

He smiled back. "You speak English?"

"Yes, among other things."

"I'm Christian. What's your name?"

"Elesin," I replied as I took his hand to shake it.

"You new to the neighborhood?"

"Yes, I just settled in with my daughter and...roommate," I answered.

"Nice to meet you. I am four houses down

that way," he pointed to a house that was in the direction of mine.

"Ah, we are practically neighbors," I smiled, hoping that I wasn't blushing too much. As our conversation progressed, he asked where I was originally from. He complimented me on my accent and my "gorgeous" green eyes. After answering his questions, I learned that Christian was a famous Puerto Rican singer who had been a part of a huge Spanish boy band when he was younger. He was now attempting to make his mark as a solo artist in the U.S.

"Yes, Christian Ayala…I've heard of you," I gushed over his sexy Spanish accent and smoldering good looks. "I guess we have a lot in common. Well, with the exception that you made a career out of singing."

"What? You sing too? Maybe you could sing for me sometime."

"Maybe, if you're lucky," I joked. We must have chatted for over an hour about the happenings in our lives. It was great. He was very easy to talk to and definitely easy on the eyes. I could see us being close friends. I needed that now, more than ever.

"Well, I have to go. I'll see you later," he said as he extended his hand. "It was really nice meeting you."

"Same here. I'll see you around." As he walked off into the direction of his home, I decided, after a few minutes, that it was time for me to head back. I was sure that Lynnea was up by now. When I got back to the house, Richard was putting the finishing touches on dinner. I was so glad he could cook. Maybe one day I'd learn, just not today.

"Smells good," I said. "What is it?"

"Vegetable lasagna and homemade garlic bread," he answered.

"Yummy, I love Italian." Actually, I love anything that tasted good. Giving Richard a nod of approval, I went to check on Lynnea. She was up and ready for some much-needed attention. I scooped her into my arms and carried her downstairs for dinner.

It was nice to sit at a table together, like a real family. That's what I desperately craved was a family, not the dysfunctional blood-related mess that I had. Richard and I would steal glances at each other as we ate and discussed our future plans. There was so much to do and with nothing to stop me, I was going to do it all.

After dinner, we all went out to the beach to hang out. I took a book to read Lynnea a story. We played in the sand, which Lynnea absolutely loved. We even splashed around in the water. It was a busy and exciting day for us all. A few hours later, I got Lynnea bathed and ready for bed. She tried to fight off the sleep but succumbed quickly. I stared at her; she is so perfect, so sweet and so mine.

As I left the room, I found Richard out on the patio with a couple of beers.

"You ready for bed?" he asked. I nodded as I took one of the brews from his hand. "Let's go shower so that I can get you all lathered up," he said with a sly grin.

I licked the rim of the beer bottle. "Ha! Okay, let's go."

Richard and I had lived together in paradise for three weeks before he had to get back to Canada. He taught me how to drive and had set me up with my own car. I took him to the airport and saw him off. That was one of the hardest things that I had to do. I was no longer in the comfort of familiar territory. I had no friends, no family – I would truly be alone, just me and Lynnea

Over the next few months, I did my best to make a comfortable life for us. Richard would call me every other day to check up on us. I would always ask if anyone had asked about me or for me. No one ever did. My mother clearly wanted nothing to do with me. My father had apparently fallen off the wagon and nobody had heard from him. No one even suspected or cared that I had been MIA.

Honestly, I don't know why I cared so much. I held a small glimmer of hope that one day my mother would show some sense of compassion or concern for my well being, but who was I kidding? The only person I'd seriously hoped would miss me and maybe even look for me was my sister, but she never did. That hurt me to the core. I had no family. I had no one, no one but Lynnea and Richard.

Chapter 6
Exploration

While Richard was away, Christian made a great companion. He absolutely loved Lynnea and she adored him. Richard met Christian a few times, but he did not like us hanging out so much. He was convinced that Christian was trying to steal me away from him. So, of course, Christian was the cause of a lot of heated arguments we had. While Richard was away, the jealousy grew even more.

Christian was nice but he was very serious all the time. I had never met anyone more driven in my life. He was brilliant and had a lot of great ideas running around in his head. We would sit out by the pool to write poetry and songs. While most of my poetry was a little too dark for him, he liked them just as much as I loved his.

Christian and I enjoyed each other's company and spent a lot of time together. There were a lot of things Christian wanted to share with me and it was he who suggested that I get an au pair.

He would say, "I know that you're a dad and all, but you are young and there is fun to be had."

"I know, but I can't have just anyone watching my girl."

"I know this agency that a few of my friends use. They cater to a more high-scaled clientele."

After some convincing, Christian helped me set up a meeting with the agency. It took me a week before I found Jaelyn, a cute, black Panamanian chick from Texas. She was twenty-years-old and had a degree in child development from the U.S. We hit it off from the start. She not only took care of Lynnea, but she took care of our home. She cooked, cleaned, went grocery shopping, and basically did everything that I hated to do.

About a year of living in Mexico, my crush on Christian grew into something more. Even though he traveled just as much as Richard, he would often invite me to join him. Lynnea and I got to see him perform on stage doing concerts, television shows and special charitable events. It was nice being included.

When he got a break, he would take me out to various bars and clubs where we could meet people and get our dance on. We met a lot of interesting people who introduced me to a whole new world.

Frisky Times was a rowdy gay bar. If you wanted to explore your wilder side, that was the place to be. I had managed to coerce Christian to go to a drag show with me at Club Picante. It was there I fell in love with club life. The dark, smoke-filled club was rocking with glittering lights moving with the pulsating beats. Drag queens roamed around taking pictures with their admirers; it was mind blowing. Being able to express myself with fashion and makeup was exciting.

Don't get me wrong, I'm not a drag queen, but I do look great as a woman. I loved being able to dress up in different costumes to change my look. One night at a themed costume party, I dressed up as Tony Manero, John Travolta's character from Saturday Night Fever. The look was very sexy, and very little was left to the imagination.

It was at karaoke night at a bar where Christian heard me sing for the first time. He and other spectators expected this glammed up, pretty blonde-haired boy to sound just as bad as the other drunken singers before him who graced the stage. To everyone's surprise, I sang the hell out of Moody Blues', "Nights in White Satin." I sang it with the heartfelt emotion it was intended to convey. That night I was filled with not only passion but Tequila—lots and lots of Tequila— and a pill I was given that I was not familiar with.

The bar patrons were all mesmerized, especially Christian. Everyone held up lighters, glasses and other items, swaying side to side. When I looked into Christian's eyes and sang to him, he never took his eyes off of me. I chose that song for a reason. I had developed strong feelings for Christian, and I wanted him to know it. I just hoped that he felt the same.

It had been about a month after our bar hopping that I was able to see Christian again. He had come over to the house to hang out while Jaelyn took Lynnea to the park. Christian decided to jump into the pool while I worked on my tan. He shared tales about what it was like to tour, the various people he'd met and the wild celebrity parties. As he continued on, I could not hear a word he said. I focused on the water that was beading off his beautiful brown chest, his beautiful lips and those arms. I wanted him bad.

I jumped into the pool to cool off as Rick sat on the steps at the opposite side of the pool. I swam under the water toward him. When I surfaced, I rose to stand in front of him. Christian always had this look on his face like he was in deep thought, concentrating on something that had been plaguing his mind for awhile.

So I asked, "What are you thinking about?"

"Nothing much."

"Really? You look like you have something to say."

Taking a deep breath, Christian attempted to answer but then shrugged it off.

"Are you thinking about me? You want me, don't you?" I joked.

Christian rolled his eyes, blushed then shook his head.

"I've just got a lot on my mind," he said, gazing into my eyes with a look of confliction.

"C'mon, just tell me."

"It's not the right time."

Pressing my chest to his, I said, "You're right. Maybe now is not the right time to talk."

I began running my hand along his chest but I said nothing.

"Elesin, what are you doing?" he asked. I gazed into his eyes, which were big as saucers. I began breathing heavy as I worked my hand down to his trunks, when suddenly he grabbed my wrists, holding on tightly.

"What are you doing?" he asked.

"Something that feels right." I pushed him against the side of the pool. His gaze was more intense as I ran my thumb across his lips. Just as he was about to respond, I pulled him in for a kiss, deep and passionate. Our bodies began grinding and rubbing against each other. I could barely breathe. He pulled my hair and allowed his lips to explore the side of my neck. My eyes rolled back with pleasure.

We continued enjoying each other's bodies. His hand slid down to my trunks and his fingers gained access to explore my ass. Then he pushed me away. "I can't do this. I'm sorry." He swam to the stairs, exited the pool and made a mad dash inside the house.

I chased after him. I couldn't believe he was denying the obvious attraction. When I finally reached him, I asked, "What's wrong?"

"I'm sorry," he apologized. "I can't do this. It's not right. What we're doing is wrong. And I am not sure that I want this..." He grabbed his keys from the counter.

"Please, don't leave."

"It's for the best." The conflict and frustration upon Christian's face was clear. He was right. We were both in relationships. He had been with his longtime girlfriend for just as long as I'd known him. Even though we were both in these semi-serious relationships, it was apparent how we felt about each other.

"No, you're staying," I said, forcing him down to the floor. I seductively ran my tongue along his lips, then thrust my crotch against his. Christian responded by rolling me over. He shoved his tongue down the back of my throat.

Finally allowing himself to be free, his tongue traveled down my chest. Then, pulling off my shorts, he forced me around and rammed his rock hard cock up my ass. I jerked with each pulsation, moaning as he pulled my hair and then nibbled my ear. I loved it when they pulled my hair. When we were finished, we lay spent on the floor, holding each other. Hours later, after we showered and enjoyed each other's time again, I kissed him good-bye.

It wasn't long after our hook-up that Christian went away to finish up his album. Since I had nothing planned, he invited me to the studio with him. "It's where the magic happens," he would say. I thought that watching him lay down a track for his album was going to be the highlight. However, there was one song in particular that he was working on that caught my attention— "Secret Lover." It was absolutely beautiful. As he continued singing, my heart melted. He looked in my direction and I knew. The song was about us.

As he came out the booth, he asked if I liked the track. He had a sly look on his face and I was speechless. I had no idea how to respond. He winked and continued to put the finishing touches on the song with his friend and producer, Daz. Afterward, he tried to coax me into going inside the booth, but I declined.

"Ah, what are you afraid of?" he'd ask.

"I'm not afraid of anything. I just don't want to embarrass you by out singing you." I quipped.

"Fah-Q you, pal."

"You wish."

"Oh, wait! We've done that already." Everyone in the studio got a kick out of our back and forth banter. Finally, after a few minutes of badgering me, I gave in.

"All right! I'll do it. What do you want to hear?"

"Sing anything. Sing what you sang at the bar."

"No, I don't want to do that one."

"Then what?" he asked as I sat and thought about what song I could sing without totally embarrassing myself. I knew that I had a pretty decent voice, but not good enough to cut demos. The only song that popped into my head was Queen's "Who Wants to Live Forever." After a few bars, I stopped. Christian, the producer and one of the writers stared, grinning from ear to ear. The look in Christian's eyes especially made me feel as if…well…it was a look I'll never forget.

"Didn't I tell you guys? His voice is amazing," Christian said.

"Thank you." I'm sure I was blushing.

"Have you ever thought about singing professionally?"

"Yeah right!"

"No, seriously. You should at least consider it. Your voice is…it just is," Christian said as he surveyed the room. The team nodded in agreement.

"That good, huh? Or are you just trying to get into my pants?" I laughed as the producer gave me the thumbs-up. Well, maybe I was that good.

Christian had suggested working with him on a few songs and getting exposure. That was the beginning of our professional relationship. I even got to sing background vocals on his promotional tours.

It wasn't too long after that that I got noticed by an agent from a well-known modeling agency. The look I had was very "exotic" and apparently in demand. Most of the jobs I booked were not very conventional. I did a lot of androgynous shoots, a lot of liner, a lot of makeup and a lot of fun. A handful of pictures were very suggestive. Those were very popular in the gay community.

I had eventually booked this huge modeling contract in Germany. Both Christian and Richard were quite happy with my new found success. While doing a runway show, it was suggested that I darken my hair "to make my eyes pop." I was now rocking chocolate brown, shoulder-length locks. I was there for three weeks doing various shows and pictorials for a sexy ad campaign

The year had gone by so fast. I was booking modeling gigs left and right. I was also frequenting a lot of clubs. Sex clubs with people dressed head to toe in latex and leather to laid back clubs with more of a bohemian feel. Needless to say, I was exposed to quite a few unique people and new locations. Before going home to my family, I took a detour in L.A. at the request of my agent Diane. She told me that someone was very interested in my "look."

"I think that it would be a great opportunity for you there. You could do so much more there," she suggested. "You should really consider relocating, making L.A. your home base."

"Okay, I'll see how Richard feels about it."

"Damn Richard. He barely lives with you anyways. Just go!" she urged.

She was right. Richard was hardly home with me anymore. He would visit from time to time, but for the most part, it was me, Lynnea and Jaelyn— one big, happy pseudo-family.

Chapter 7
L.A.

I had been invited to a private party in West Hollywood to meet and greet with some important people in the industry; real movers and shakers who could make or break one's career. It was at this party where I would have my chance meeting with a record producer. I walked the room with confidence that everyone seemed to notice, especially the ladies.

I was working my tight black satin button down shirt and a bright pink pair of pants and heavy black eye liner. I could make an impression no matter where I was. As I made my rounds through the various rooms, I noticed a gorgeous woman tending bar. Her skin was like black velvet, so silky that I almost reached out to touch her. I know...very tacky.

She had beautiful almond-shaped brown eyes and she was working a nice asymmetrical shoulder length bob. I notice everything. She had many male admirers vying for her attention, but somehow I managed to make eye contact with her and I beckoned her over to my side of the bar.

"What can I get for you?" she asked in a very sexy voice, sliding a napkin in front of me.

"What do you suggest?"

"Depends."

"On?"

"Are you a sweet man?" she paused, looking me up and down with her eyes. "Strong or a little bit of both?" I felt as if she were speaking in some sort of code, trying to figure out which team I batted for.

"I guess I like a little bit of everything. Surprise me," I answered with a big sly smile on my face.

She winked and giggled. "I got something for you."

As she began mixing things together like a mad scientist of cocktails, I looked around the bar as some of the men were glaring at me. Then I turned my attention back to the pretty bartender. Damn! I just kept thinking that I could so nail that. Those curves...those lips...Hmm! Maybe I'm bi after all.

"Here ya go, sweetie," she said, handing me my drink.

I took a sip. "Wow, that's deadly," I said. "Any more drinks like that and I'll think that you're trying to take me home."

"Well, maybe I am." She winked. "How am I doing so far?"

I gave a wink and said, "Just say the word and I'm yours." We both laughed as she went back to work the bar. Looking down at the number written on the napkin by my drink, I folded it up and stuffed it in my pants pocket. I swiveled around on the stool, taking notice of the men at the bar. They represented ages twenty-one to fifty-nine, all nationalities and all with the same looks of envy and shock. I tipped my glass to the bar patrons, hopped off the stool and left to check out the rest of the place.

My agent, Diane found me hanging out on the patio, with a record producer following close at her heels. In L.A., it was never too hard to spot a talent agent or a record producer. They seemed to carry an air of cockiness, wore designer watches and had an electronic device in their hands. The look of a predator searching for prey. Even when not dressed in tailored designer suits, they all shared that same look.

The look of determination to score the next talent and Neal Diamond was no different. Although he was in his mid-fifties with thinning gray tussled hair, and wore thin gold framed glasses, he was intimidating. He wasn't in the best shape but his talents were always fit.

"Elesin, I'd like you to meet Neal Diamond. He's a producer from Intercontinental Records."

Neal extended his hand to mine. "I'm so glad to finally meet you. I've heard so many wonderful things about you," he said.

"Oh, really? What kind of things?"

"Some friends of mine say that you have an amazing voice. I've also heard some demos and agree that you are a great talent. I also think that you would be great for a group I am putting together."

"Oh?"

He handed me a card. "I'd love to talk with you more about this project of mine. Call my assistant Marci to set up the meeting. I'll like to get this thing off the ground by the end of the year." He gave me a few more details about the all boy band group he was creating. "I want a diverse group of young men who are soulful, talented white boys. Sort of an updated New Kids on the Block."

"Okay, well, let me stop you there." I interrupted. "I am not white nor am I American."

"Not a problem. I am all about creating an image," he said. "People believe in what they see. So what are you? Like Creole or what?"

"Sort of, mother is black, African actually, and my father is white." The look of shock that ran across his face was priceless. You would have thought that I had told him that I shot a political figure.

"Okay." He nodded. "That is not going to be a problem. Again, it's all about image. In the end, it's all about marketing. If people assume that you're white, so be it. Besides, the group does not have to be promoted as an all-American white boy band. We'll discuss more during our meeting." He continued as he kept he gaze on me. I'm sure he was trying to figure out how I looked the way I did, perhaps how he could market me. The wheels were definitely turning. We ended our conversation with another handshake and said our good-byes.

After the party, my agent and I left to get some coffee and talk business. We found a Starbucks and chatted about the people we met and plans she had for me for the month.

"Elesin, you should really think about expanding your career options. You're in L.A. You have a look that would be suited for not only print ads but television as well." She continued explaining possible career options as she nibbled on her low-fat blueberry loaf. I continued to listen closely to all she had to say.

"When you meet with Neal, really pay attention to him. He could get you so much exposure that it could really catapult you to places you could only dream of."

I listened to her wondering if I could be a part of this great "American" boy band. Could that really happen? Then, what if it does? How could this affect me...my family? What if someone found out about my past? Would they care? I shrugged the thought off. I guess we'd just have to see.

Diane was gabbing a mile a minute, selling me on Neal and the potential impact on my future in entertainment.

"I'm in. Let's set up the meeting as soon as possible," I interrupted. She was beaming with excitement. Quickly, she dug into her Coach purse, retrieved her palm pilot and made a note to set up a meeting with Neal's assistant.

As she did that, I took in the moment thinking of my life and the many fortunate opportunities I had. I was actually happy. And just thinking about my beautiful daughter made it all worth it. Taking in the night, I sipped my toffee nut latte, extra hot with whip, of course.

Once I made it back to Mexico, I called Christian who was working on his crossover album in L.A. When I told him I was moving to L.A., he was so excited, especially when shared the news about my scheduled meeting with Neal Diamond, thee Neal Diamond, and how I was being scouted for a boy band. Christian got a kick out of that.

"So where in L.A. will you be working?" he asked.

"I have no idea. My agent is getting everything set up. We'll be gone within three weeks, though."

"Three weeks! Wow! That's so soon," he said. "Good luck to you."

"Thanks. We'll have to celebrate when you get back."

"Oh yes, we will."

The stars were definitely aligning. Christian and I would both be working in L.A.

Chapter 8
I'm with the Band

The meeting with Neal Diamond was set up for two weeks after the party where I met him. He had been recruiting talented young men from all over the United States to get the look and sound for this group. The meeting was a bit informal, very casual actually. He wanted to skip the pleasantries and five minutes after I arrived he ushered me into the booth to sing. According to him, he needed to get an idea where my voice would fit within the band. To me, the sample tracks were a bit cheesy, but when you think about it, the whole boy band thing was a hot, cheesy mess. Nonetheless, I hit my notes with perfection.

Afterwards, it was back to his office to question me about my life. I was actually honest with him, for the most part. I told him about my situation and how I came to the U.S., omitting, of course, the disgusting and illegal details. He sat with raised eyebrows, taking in everything I was saying. Then he changed the subject, obviously noticing my smudged eyeliner from the night before.

"So, would you say that you are more of a punk rock guy or a fashion guy?" he asked, as he looked me up and down, checking out my fitted black, striped trousers, tight black button down, short sleeved shirt. "I only ask because I notice that you have, uh, eye liner? And is that glitter?" he asked.

"Yeah, I wear liner sometimes. And yes, that is glitter, when I go to clubs, you know? Glitter is hard to get off sometimes," I answered with a smile. "I don't consider myself a rocker guy. I guess I am into fashion."

"But, you do it for fun? You're not a cross dresser, right?"

"Ah...well, not exactly. But I have dressed up as a woman before." I chuckled as he processed what I shared.

"Well, I'm sure it was all in fun. However, the image I would like to have for this group needs to represent the great American ideal of a boy band. Wholesome, Christian...well as close to it as possible. I want boys that every girl dreams of and every mother secretly lusts after." He went on, stressing how deviation from that dream band would be detrimental to the plan.

He wanted the appearance of all "straight" boys. For the sake of getting myself into the group I figured I could play straight. He also suggested that I once I joined, I should meet with a speech coach in order to lessen my thick French accent. He thought it would be interesting to keep a bit of the accent, just not so much. He wanted to make people want to know more about me without giving out too much information about myself or my identity.

He removed his thin, gold-framed glasses and said, "Does this sound like something you could be a part of?"

"Yes! It does."

"Great! Oh yeah, how old are you? Like nineteen?"

"Um, I'm twenty-one." The lie rolled right off my tongue as I continued lying about my age. He caught me off guard because I was actually nineteen-years-old and he had me pegged. I shook it off and continued to answer more questions regarding my life. I told him about my daughter and my non-traditional living situation with Richard. He paused for a moment and then shrugged his shoulders and said that as long as my boyfriend did not interfere with record sales, I could sleep with whomever I wanted.

He reclined in his leather chair, kicked up his feet on the mahogany desk and asked more questions about my parents and how estranged we were. As I talked about my upbringing and the difficult time I had with my racial identity, he nodded with understanding. He reassured me that most families were in some way estranged and that my situation should not be a problem.

"El, can I call you El?" I shrugged, even though I hated when people shortened my name. He continued, "Like I said before, it's all about image and dollars. If it doesn't make dollars, it doesn't make sense."

The rest of the meeting was more or less a quick overview about the company and the acts produced. It was very apparent that Neal had the golden touch or the diamond and double platinum touch. Before ending the meeting, he went over his expectations of me and the other band mates. He wanted to get the selected young men together and have the group up and recording in two months and touring in six. He set a pretty aggressive schedule but was sure it was doable.

As Neal walked me and my agent to the main lobby, he thanked me for my time and had his assistant give my agent a contract to read over.

"It's pretty standard," he stated and winked. He extended his hand to mine and shook it was a strong grip. I thanked him for the opportunity and went on my way.

Outside, the most beautiful sunny skies welcomed me. I looked up and asked myself, "Is this something I can really do?" After a brief moment I pumped my fist in the air and yelled. "Hell yeah!" It took about week to go over the contract with my lawyer and make revisions.

During that time, Christian had almost completed his second solo album. On the rare occasion Christian had some free time, I would invite him to an underground drag club I found and frequented regularly. It was there I began experimenting with more drugs, men and women. I did not discriminate. This new lifestyle did not sit well with Richard who now wanted to live full time with me in L.A.

I got really caught up in the club life in L.A. I submerged myself in the culture, the eclectic fashion, the sex and the bullshit that came with life as a club boy. It wasn't long before settling in our home in L.A. that I began to get favorable attention from both men and women. Richard did not like that too much. He began to have jealous rages and took out his frustration on my body. Even at five feet, eleven inches, I was no match for a six-three, two hundred pound man who was built like a prized fighter, not exactly a fair fight.

Although Richard would hurt me, I could take it. Unlike the beatings I would take from Sebastian, Richard acted out of love and was typically followed by an apology, flowers or some sort of gift. His anger was justified, after all, if I didn't sleep around or betray his trust he wouldn't have cause to hit me.

Fortunately, he would avoid hitting me in the face since that was the money maker. I still had a very lucrative modeling career to protect and maintain. However, there were times when I would have to cancel important meetings due to Richard and his abuse on my body.

I'd be so badly beaten that there was no way that I could hide the bruises. I turned to cocaine to numb the pain. I was already doing lines, a little something I picked up from the clubs, but the beatings increased my usage.

It wasn't long before I began developing a bad reputation due to missing jobs. Modeling was a very temperamental business. Being just thirty seconds late could piss some people off and have you black listed. I had become labeled a diva in the modeling world, but I was still in demand.

As my music career began to take off and Richard increasingly using me as his personal punching bag, Jaelyn would be my buffer and made life and work easier to cope with. She was my refuge from all the bad shit I had to deal with. With her, I had more freedom to be me. I also had less to worry about with her around.

Jaelyn was a comfort to me. It was only natural that she and I would become lovers. I think Richard suspected something was going on between Jealyn and me but he didn't say anything. If he knew for certain he definitely would not approve. There were times when he looked at me and it was as if I were staring into the eyes of a stranger. The man I loved was good and kind but he was fast becoming the man I feared.

I enjoyed the time Jaelyn and I spent together. I enjoyed kissing her, holding her and loving her. It felt right, it was different than what I had with Richard – it was nurturing. I was never afraid that she'd hurt me or that she would ever cross me.

She was all about taking care of Lynnea and me. I never wanted to let that go. I'd even had thoughts – that it would be easy for me to love her. Life with Jaelyn could make my life better. We could be the family that I've always dreamed of having...the life that I'd always wanted.

Neal finally handpicked the ideal group. He wanted us to be these wholesome boy-next-door types that the girls would swoon over and the mothers would lust after. Neal wanted me and the guys to work closely together and rented out this mansion for us to stay in while we got the group up and running.

I had to leave Richard and the girls behind while Marci, Neal's assistant was finding a new home for my family. Meanwhile, my new home with the band was awesome; it had a pool, gym and a built-in studio.

I was the first to arrive at the mansion. I was lounging out by the pool when I met my first house-mate, Monte James, better known as MJ. He was the youngest at eighteen-years-old. He was this skinny, curly blonde-haired, blue-eyed boy from Texas. He was a prankster but he was fun to be around. I liked him right away. I could be a kid with him.

The next two arrived later that afternoon.

Jasper (Jazz) Delveccio was the twenty-two-year-old Italian stud…his description, not mine. He had dark brown, almost black, hair, brown eyes and several tattoos and was kind of scary looking at first sight. He was brash and crude and had no problems speaking his mind.

Zack Marsh was just weird. He was a short twenty-year old, dark-haired wannabe hip hopper with the brightest blue eyes I'd ever seen. He was loud and loved to speak in a slang that no one could understand.

Last to arrive was Chace Hamilton, this nineteen-year-old pretty boy from Malibu with light brown hair with blonde highlights. Upon sight, I knew I'd probably get along with him really well. He had a great fashion sense and I think I caught him checking me out a few times.

Once everyone was settled and got the formal intros out of the way, Neal organized a catered meal for us and sat with us and reiterated his expectations for his group. We all gathered around the large rectangular mahogany dinner table while being served. We listed as Neal established some harsh rules to live by while in the house.

"I don't put up with any bullshit. You're late to a meeting, rehearsal or anything that requires you and your band-mates for even a minute…and you will be fined, heavily."

We all squirmed unable to settle ourselves in our chairs, shooting quick glances at each other as he continued on.

"You can have fun but I don't want any calls from jail or you will have hell to pay."

The next morning we learned just how serious Neal was about the rules and regulations he had for us. At five thirty in the morning, he not only put us on a strict curfew but a strict workout regiment as well which included a personal trainer from hell.

The Russian assassin looked to be about seven-feet-tall and barely spoke a word of English but could bark out orders. Poor Chace passed out after the first fifteen minutes of training. I was holding my own but at one point, it felt as if I was having an asthma attack, and I don't even have asthma.

Once the Russian torturer was done with us after a grueling two-hour sessions, two of us fell out, the others managed to crawl to the bathrooms for a steamy, hot shower. Then, it was off to choreography. Needless to say, I was exhausted. After about three weeks of this crash course of being sculpted into this super band, we headed to the studios to lay tracks and focus on our first single.

A month and a half later, our sound was being fine tuned and we were ready to promote. We definitely had a few songs that would be hits. We were so excited. Neal even gave us a few days off to let off some steam.

I called Richard over and he brought along Lynnea and Jaelyn who was now showing at six months. It was great to see the people I loved. Lynnea was especially happy to see her dad and could not contain her excitement. She was so chatty and so smart for a three year old. The boys and their friends and family just adored her.

Jazz, the most vocal of the group, pointed out Jaelyn's noticeable baby bump. "What's going on here?"

Jaelyn giggled, "Yeah, I'm getting so big." She was bombarded with questions left and right.

"Do you know if it's a boy or girl?"

"Have you picked a name?"

"Who's the father? Are getting married?"

Jaelyn handled herself well, answering everyone's questions with a smile on her face as she tried not to out me as the father. Richard was getting annoyed by all the inquiries regarding the nature of the relationship I had with Jaelyn. He was especially annoyed when I introduced him as my long-time friend and roommate. He was ready to leave.

"Let's go grab some dinner," Richard suggested.

"Yeah, that would be great." It had been awhile since we'd seen each other and had a meal together. Before taking off, Richard wanted some alone time with me so I lead him to my room.

"So we're alone, what did you want to do?" I asked.

"Well, I kind of wanted to talk about us," he said as he sat on the corner of my bed.

"Us what?" I asked with curious ears.

"Well, I know that you are young and about to be exposed to a lot more, uh, experiences and opportunities. And..." he stared down to the floor, obviously searching for the correct words to say. "I love you and I always have, Elesin."

"Same here."

"Yes, I know you do. But I understand that you'll get lonely and you'll want to have lots of fun...and sex," he continued.

"What are you trying to say?"

"What I am trying to say is that you are free to have sex with other people and experience all that life has to offer you. All I ask is that when you are home with me, I am the only one you have a relationship with." Taking my hand in his, he continued, "I know you are young and deserve to experience all that life has to offer but I want you to promise that I will be your only relationship."

"Okay, I promise." I smiled as I pulled him up and into my arms. "You will be my only relationship." He smiled and leaned in to kiss my lips. Even though Jaelyn was having my child, Richard chalked that up to me being foolish and being a kid. I knew deep down that Richard did not like that idea of me bedding other men – women. But I got the impression that he felt in order to keep from losing me he would need to loosen his grasp on me.

Even though he beat the shit out of me after he found out about me and Christian, I knew that he still loved me. I did not ever want to upset him like that again; especially after all he's done for me. I owed him my life.

Richard and I made love on my bed as I laid in his arms, I could not shake the feeling that I was making a huge mistake—a mistake in promising him that I would be true, a mistake in me not telling him that Christian was also in L.A. and I thought that I was falling for my Latin lover. That would just break Richard's heart and I just didn't want to know what he would do to me if he knew.

As we returned to the living room, my band mates and guests were still chatting and beginning to set off for their own plans. When Richard and I returned to the living room and no one seemed to suspect anything more about our relationship than what I shared. I had never disclosed my sexual orientation with my band-mates but I wasn't exactly in the closet.

I didn't care if they knew that I was sleeping with both men and women, but I just didn't feel that they were ready. After chatting it up with the boys and their guests, Richard led Jaelyn, Lynnea and me off to dinner.

We dined at California Pizza Kitchen and shared a roasted garlic chicken pizza. The conversations were nice as we sat amongst the rows of feasting patrons who were also enjoying light conversations and a decent meal. Surprisingly it was almost as if we were all a real family, enjoying each other's company.

After awhile, we talked of my schedule with the band. Jaelyn was all too excited about me and my new career path, and was especially excited about me working with Jazz, the Italian stud.

"Are you close with Jazz? What's he like behind the scene?"

"Yeah, what's he like?" Richard asked with suspicion.

When Richard chimed in, for some reason it felt more like an inquisition than friendly chit chat. I got visibly flushed and rubbed my hands on my thighs. Of all the people to pick out, he gets suspicious of the six-foot-tall Italian stud. If he were not so obnoxious or straight, then I would be even more nervous with Richard's interest in my relationship with the boys.

"Well, he's okay. He's really brash and opinionated."

"Do you boys get along?" she asked.

"For the most part. I mean, we haven't had too much time to bond yet."

Richard squinted as if something were weighing on his mind. "So, is there someone in the group that you are close with or feel that you would be close to?"

"Richard, don't."

"I'm just curious."

"Babe, you don't have to worry about them. Besides, I'm pretty sure that I'm the only one who likes handsome men." Richard leaned back into his chair, staring at me intensely. "Seriously babe. Don't worry about it. Please."

"Okay, then I won't. Anyone want desert?"

Lynnea was the only one enthused about having dessert as Jaelyn and I looked awkwardly down at our plates.

After dinner, Richard took Jaelyn and Lynnea back to hotel. I kissed my baby girls goodnight as I watched them enter the hotel through the huge glass doors of the Omni Los Angeles Hotel at California Plaza.

Richard drove me back to the house in silence. Richard walked me up to the door and took me into his arms...not wanting to let me go. He leaned in to kiss me good bye and wished me well. Richard drove me back to the house. He held me in his arms, not wanting to let me go.

"I'll miss you."

"I'll miss you too Richard. Please just trust me."

"I'm really trying to be understanding. Just give me time to adjust this whole thing. I mean, you could become a huge star and then – who knows what'll happen, to us."

"Baby, nothing is going to happen to us. We will be fine. I promise." Richard gave me a big squeeze, nestling my neck with his nose. I could feel him inhaling, taking me into his soul. I closed my eyes, remembering what it was like before the jealousy, before Mexico. Then he kissed me good bye and wished me well.

Chapter 9
Revelation

My band mates and I were getting ready to make our rounds to promote our new album and upcoming shows. The car picked us up from the mansion at nine to take us to our meet and greet at the Grove in Los Angeles. As we sat at our tables, Zack leaned over towards me with a curious look in his eyes.

I could hardly focus on his facial expressions as his newly acquired mini dreadlocks that pointed in every direction diverted my attention.

"So, did you and Richard have fun last night?"

"Of course we did. Why wouldn't we?" It was really hard hard to take Zack seriously with his multi-colored dreadlocks. Somehow, he coordinated them with his brightly colored oversized t-shirt and baggy shorts.

"Uh-hum." I knew immediately where his line of question was headed after overhearing both Jazz and Zack talking about my demeanor with Richard. My band-mates were not sure of my sexual orientation but had their suspicion. No one ever asked me directly but would ask me in a roundabout way.

"Do you like show tunes?"

"Are you into cross-dressing?"

"How do you feel about Barbara Streisand?"

I was not sure why they just didn't ask me directly? However, after my responses, there were even more baffled. I mean, I wasn't crazy about show tunes and I like sports. I loved hockey, rugby and soccer but as far as Barbara, she's an amazingly talented woman. I absolutely loved her in the movie Nuts but I prefer a classic like Donna Summer.

Jazz ran his fingers through his solidly gelled hair and was about to say something but stopped.

"Is there something on your minds?" I asked as they eyeballed each other.

"Well, now that you've mentioned it." Jazz noted as he came in closer to me. "Are you and Richard like a couple?" Waiting for a response, Zack leaned in and mouthed, "Are you gay?"

I could not help but to laugh. The other band mates looked on waiting for me to come out to them.

"Well, let's just say that my heart could belong to either a man or a woman." The look of confusion was even more evident on their faces.

Then MJ asked, "So, if you and Richard are boyfriends, then what is Jaelyn to you? She is having your baby--right?"

They had obviously been doing their homework in investigating me.

"I prefer to call Richard my domestic partner." I smirked as the lines began to get set up with potential fans wanting autographs and pictures.

But that did not stop the firing squad of questions.

"Who's the chick in the relationship?"

"Do you take it up the ass?"

"How long have you been gay?"

"Do you swallow?"

I looked around for reporters who were always hanging in the wings waiting for a scoop. I saw none so without hesitation, I answered every single question by the time the first potential fan reached us.

"We are two men, yes, my whole life and of course." The looks on their faces were priceless. The shock--the terror, I wished that I had a camera.

The guys then looked at each other and with a nod, Jazz said, "Okay! I can live with that. It's all good." The rest of the guys nodded in approval as well.

"Good! You have no idea how much I needed your approval to feel complete."

The remainder of the meet and greet when really well and seamless. After about an hour of signing autographs and taking pictures with the potential fans; it was time to get set up for our performance. We were to perform two songs. A select few got a sample CD with the songs that were being performed.

While on the stage, I got really nervous. This was totally different from the drag shows that I had performed in the past. This was more real. This was me.

MJ leaned over to me with fear in his eyes and said, "I am scared shitless." After that, I reassured him that we would do just fine. The song began--we hit our marks perfectly. The crowd roared. The rush...nothing could explain that feeling. I could really get use to *this*, I thought to myself.

Over the next few weeks, this became routine. A buzz about our group was making its rounds. Some air play on the radio, then the tour. We got to start for Tiffy Stone. She was this hot pop star who was at the top of every chart you could think of. She was starting a fifty two city tour to promote her new album. We were doing ton of interviews for magazines, radio and television.

By the tenth interview and answering the same questions over and over again, we were exhausted. Somehow, we donned our fake smiles and gave polished answers to the questions being asked.

"Do you have girlfriends?"

"How do you all get along?"

"How does it feel to have screaming girls throwing themselves at you?"

Naturally, to our fans we were all eligible bachelors who all got along and loved our adoring fans. If the fans only knew the truth; they'd know that both Jazz and I were in serious relationships and MJ was "secretly" dating a fellow female pop star; however, we all had to seem available to our female fans from a sales standpoint.

Within months of interviewing and touring, we were surpassing Tiffy's popularity on her own tour. N'Step had become household names. After Tiffy's U.S. tour, she went on to conquer Europe and we were headlining our own tour. I just could not believe how fast the fame came about. I could not have asked for anything more.

The touring schedule was chaotic but exciting. After another six months, we finally got a well deserved break. Richard was away on business when I arrived home to a new addition my clan. While I was on tour, Jaelyn gave birth to Jerrod, my little man.

My life was moving pretty fast, before I knew it my children where getting so big. Lynnea had been a great big sister and Jaelyn was a great mother to both of my kids. Lynnea was almost four and Jerrod nearly one already. I tried to spend every free moment I had with my babies.

Jaelyn was picking up the toys from the living area.

"Your hair it's so blue!"

"I know right." I got bored one day and decided that I did not like how I looked and dyed my hair, again. This was a more drastic change from the chocolate brown hair that she was used too. She had just barely gotten used to my hair being dark brown.

"Look's awesome though," she complimented.

"So, let me take you guys out to dinner," I suggested. Both Jaelyn and Lynnea were thrilled to go somewhere with me for a meal. Jerrod just smiled. "Wow! I don't even think that he realizes that I am his father. That will all change. I will make sure that he knows who I am. Unlike the man who--well...who cares about that."

It was nice spending quality time with my--

family. After dinner, Lynnea wanted to go to the park. It was still light outside so we were able run around a bit. Soon it had gotten dark. We loaded the kids up into the car and once we got within two blocks of our house. One of my songs began playing on the radio.

"Oh my God! You guys are everywhere." Jaelyn said with excitement. "Your group is like an updated version of The New Kids on the Block." All I could do was roll my eyes at the thought. Besides--I don't think that we could ever get that big. Could we?

While home, I put the kids to bed, read a bed time story. I smiled as my daughter read some of the words to me. It was a nice moment. Once the children were asleep, I made my way down the stairs. Jaelyn had poured us a glass of wine and we sat down on the sofa with our drinks in hand.

"So we have a whole week to ourselves." I said, running my fingers through her hair.

"Whatever are we going to do with our time together?" She asked with a coy smile on her face. Leaned over to me and kissed me. Man, did I miss those soft, tender kisses. I could not control my lust for her--ripping off her shirt. My lips exploring every part of her body. I took her...right there, on the sofa.

Lying there, with her in my arms, I wondered if I could love her. Is this life--with her, something that I could do? Could I make a real family with her? She was after all the mother of my son as well as a mother to my daughter has ever known. Jaelyn and I had the best relationship and I could share almost anything and everything with her. Who am I kidding? It would not be fair to put Jaelyn in that situation. Me tramping around with men--and some women, so I made sure not to lead her on anymore than usual.

Over the next few days, I decided to find Jaelyn a house somewhere where she could raise our children while I was busy working. She had an interest in moving closer to her family who had lived in Texas. After some calls, we were on a plane to view some houses.

Jaelyn was all too happy to set up a permanent residence near her family. She was also eager to create a safe and secure home for both Jerrod and Lynnea. I was lucky that Jaelyn loved Lynnea as if she were her own. I even asked if she would become the legal guardian over Lynnea. She thought that I was a fool for even having to ask.

As we continued looking at houses, I thought about having a safe place to go when Richard would beat the shit out of me came to mind. Why I just don't--can't leave him?
At least this way, my children would always be protected. I just could not risk Richard taking out his frustrations on my children. *I should just leave him. Why can't I just leave him?* I thought to myself.

The realtor snapped me back to reality when she said, she "You and you wife are going to love it here. This is a great place to raise your children." Jaelyn and I both laugh but never correcting the agent. After viewing several houses, Jaelyn and I decided to take the kids to McDonald's for lunch.

There they could play around and Jaelyn and I could talk. Jaelyn suggested that we should get married and raise our children in a semi normal environment.

We watched the children playing around for a few minutes before Jaelyn offered up a suggestion...getting married. She wanted to raise our children in a semi-normal environment. I almost choked off of my chocolate shake. She sat quietly stirring her French fry into the ketchup that was placed on her hamburger wrapper.

"I understand that you and Richard are together, but I think that since we do care for each other...well, in case something happens to you, it would be easier for the kids."

I took a bite of my Cheeseburger, pondering what life would be like as a "married" man. All I could do was smile at Jaelyn as she continued to make her point as to why we should be married.

"We could have an open marriage. I will never want to change who you are."
Wow! A marriage on paper, with all the perks and the lifestyle of a free wheelin' rockstar.

"That doesn't seem fair to you. I mean. I wouldn't mind being married to you but what about..."

"The men?" She answered.

"Yeah. What about them?"

"I know that you have a fondness for...uh..."

"Dick!"

"Yeah! Dick...all that I ask is that you promise to take care of your family. Protect yourself and us," she ended.

Everything she said made sense at that moment so I said, "Let's do it then."

She smiled and took my hands into hers. By the end of our meal, Jaelyn had decided on a house. She chose a modest colonial influenced style, two story house with ivy running around the frame. Iron fencing, with a rose garden. The house included six bedrooms, a game room and pool. I was cozy. I liked it.

We called the realtor to tell her that we wanted to make an offer. Then I followed up the call to my accountant to establish and account for Jaelyn so that she and my children could live comfortably.

Friction between me and my group began to get strained with my increasing popularity over the next few years. The guys, with the exception of Chace, were showing signs of jealousy and were clearly annoyed with the public's interest in me. MJ was especially hostile with me since the rumor started circulating about me sleeping with his girlfriend and my close friend, Tiffy Stone. If it weren't for Christian allowing me to vent in his each during odd hours of the day, I'd lose my mind. He was always there for me no matter what.

It always amazes me at how at the press discovers celebrity indiscretion...no matter how discrete, especially, when it was never a planned event. Tiffy and I loved the night life and enjoyed our sleep overs when her love MJ was away visiting family. One drunken and drug induced night, Tiffy and I had a one night tryst, but we vowed to never let it happen again.

The Globe ran a story with the headline 'Tiffy Stone Double Stepping within N'Step' and it insinuated that America's darling was pregnant so all hell broke loose. Tiffy started keeping her distance from me at the request of her management team. But even through the media shit storm, we were able to maintain our friendship and our vow of silence. It was just another fling that happened while I was high on life – literally.

My intake of illegal narcotics had increased due to the amount of stress I was under to keep a squeaky clean image. I was growing tired of being in the closet and having everyone speculating about me. While touring, I had been warned numerous times by management to "keep the pilot light off," and "to keep the heels in the closet, for now."

At this point during the tour, I had no idea what city I was in or what I was doing on stage. I was so messed up that I actually collapsed on the stage. Fortunately for me, it was reported that it was due to exhaustion but my band-mates knew the truth.

Somewhere in the northeast, Chace and I decided to stay in for the night while the others went out for a night on the town. I think that Chace was just trying to keep an eye on me and make sure that I did not over do it with the pharmaceuticals.

We sat out on the balcony watching the stars. Chace was looking particularly good tonight. He looked as if he stepped out of a surfer catalog with his bleach blonde highlights and tanned skinned. He was sporting khaki cargo pants that complimented his bubble butt and a t-shirt that fit like a glove.

I knew that Chace had a major crush on me but I never acted on it. Although he never came out to me, I just knew that like me, he liked the boys. Chace had declined many of my advances but on this night – he yielded. I led him to my room, and pushed him up against the coffee colored wall. We kissed feverishly, releasing all the built up tension inside of us. Then he stopped.

"What's wrong?" I asked.

"You know how I feel about you, right?" He panted.

"Well, sure. I guess." I was more confused than ever. My breathing was still heavy from the lip service I received.

"Before this happens, I want you to know one thing," he said as he led me backwards towards my bed and pushing me back. As he straddled me and began kissing me gently, he continued to say, "I know more about you than you think, but I'd like to know more."

"Okay, whatever you like," I answered. I tried to remove his shirt but was quickly stopped as he grabbed my hands and placed them over my head.

"First of all, I'm not some young trick that you can fuck over. I know the game you play and I can't help the way I feel about you." He stated as he removed my shirt and grinded against my crotch. My mind went blank, the excitement of this moment too much for me that I could barely comprehend. Chace started up again by saying, "I know that I will never be your boyfriend but I'd expect you to respect me and be honest with me. I can be your best friend or – your worst enemy. Don't fuck with me."

"Fair enough," I muttered as he continued removing my clothing. He reached into his pocket and retrieved his wallet, then pulled out a condom. "What? Don't you trust me?"

He leaned in to kiss me, ripped open the condom package and placed it on my dick, removed his clothing slowly and seductively. As he placed me inside of him, leaned into my ear he said, "Not really."As he continued to ride the shit out of me, he made himself came loud and hard.

We laid there after basking in the afterglow of our union. His fingers ran up and down my arm as he laid on top of me as he continued asking me questions.

"Vollan? That's Scandinavian right?"

"Yeah."

"But your accent is French, so where are you from originally?"

I turned my body to face him and began kissing his neck trying to deflect his questions, it didn't work.

"Well?" he asked.

"I was born in Montreal, Canada but my mother is African from Mauritius where I was raised."

"Ah! I see it now." He smirked slyly as he pushed me off of him. Making his way to the door grabbed a blanket and covered himself as he made his way to the door.

"Ah, what?"

"I was just curious to know a little bit more about you," he said as he opened the door. I rose out of bed to meet him at the door.

"So, do you feel that you know who I am?"

He smiled and said, "I just wanted to know the real you and not the you that you put on for show. I like the good side of you and wish you'd embrace it."

I smiled and leaned in to kiss him goodnight.

As Chace turned away, Jazz was standing behind him in shock with a glass of milk in one hand and a plate of cake in the other. As Chace walked by, he took his finger through the icing, placed his finger into his mouth seductively and said, "I do love me some French vanilla." Once Chace made it to his room, Jazz shook his head and made his way to his room. I laughed and went back to bed.

Dodging our handlers had begun to turn into a sort of competition between me and my bandmates. Sometimes I would disappear anywhere from an hour or sometimes depending on the venue. During this trip, I left and returned just in time for dress rehearsals then disappeared from my bandmates and staff an hour before show time.

While hiding out in one of the female restrooms, I was getting my makeup done, thick with liner and very smoky eye by my stylist Ra'mon. He added glitz and some spritz to ensure that I was fierce. I absolutely adored abnormally tall black guy from Queens who had the most "fabulous" and daring style. And yes, we ended up in bed on quite a few occasions. In just a few months he'd become very aware of my moods, so after inquiring about my sour attitude.

I looked up at him from the sink were I sat as he continued layering the liner as I decided to confide in him.

"I sometime feel forced into being something that I'm not. And it's frustrating…"

"Well, that's what you signed up for honey. That cookie cutter image that Neal loves to market." I looked Ra'mon up and down admiring his daring style. Even at six-foot-three, he was never afraid to rock a pair of the highest heels.

He leaned against the dingy white tiled wall across from me with his arms crossed.

"You know white boys who can sing and dance sale."

"I know, I know. I agreed to represent this ideal 'white straight male' but it's so stressful. I'm so confused. I don't even know who I am anymore," I pouted and continued, "I just want to be able to not worry about every single detail and making sure that it's P.C. I don't want to have every part of me exposed to the masses—just some of it."

"And we all know that you love to expose yourself," he snickered.

"Manwhore!"

We shared a good laugh as he proceeded to walk over to offer me more words of wisdom, "Baby, just do you. Don't let anyone dictate how you run your life. And don't give anyone too much power over you because they'll leave your ass up and face down on a come stained floor of a bathhouse."

I rolled my eyes as his high pitched cackle bounced off every wall as he flipped the collar of his mesh shirt.

"Nice…great visual," I said as I slid off the sink counter, laughing so hard that I was in tears. Once I got my look together, I was off to join my band-mates. The long walk down the dark corridor allowed me to reflect on all the decisions I had made up until this moment. The strength it took for me to leave home at a young age with my daughter while managing a successful modeling career and now—pop star. What the hell was I complaining about?

Apparently everyone had been scrambling to find me, so we could all get on our marks. I appeared just in time for our grand entrance. My baseball cap was lowered just enough to hide my eyes. As the lights hit, I threw the hat off into the audience. The jumbotron zoomed in on my over exaggerated eyes. We did our routine to one of our number-one hits from our first album. I added an extra swing and bounce to some of my movements and slinked seductively across the stage.

By the third song, I removed my button-down shirt, exposing my bare chest. The crowd roared. The more I sashayed across the stage the more they ate it up. While some of the guys pulled girls up on stage to sing to, I began to stumble across the stage. My body felt so heavy and tingly that I began missing key marks and forgetting lyrics. Then everything went black...I collapsed and had to be rushed to the hospital.

Not only were the guys pissed but so was our publicist Janet. I was consistently making her job difficult with my partying ways. She scrambled to cover up the episode as extreme fatigue, which was true this time around but not everyone was buying it.

The shit had hit the proverbial fan and the press was eating up my apparent drunkenness. The shit had hit the proverbial fan in Seattle, Washington. I just loved the headlines. "Elesin No Longer N'Step" and "Vollan Has Fallen." I have to admit, I liked that one. My behavior on stage was the topic of every television news show and talk show. Some of the hosts and guests were not shocked by the incident and felt that it was typical of a young entertainer. But others were not amused and found it to be offensive.

Neal and the management team were mortified that I was being careless with my appearance and my performances. Can you say emergency meeting? Neal had flown up with the management team, our publicists and legal before our next concert. Needless to say, Neal was very disappointed and frustrated with my lack of professionalism. We were all gathered in a conference room at the hotel we were staying at in Detroit.

"What the hell were you thinking?" I just sat silent, shrugging my shoulders. "Whatever it was, I hope that it is out of you system now."

He went on and on about family values and being careless with my dick, drugs and the band's reputation. *Blah, blah, fucking blah, blah.* I still had no response not getting a response and Neal looked to the other guys to help out with the why. When no one answered, he continued on, "By your reaction, it would seem that you are upset with something?" Or is this something we need to take care of in rehab?" Neal huffed.

I continued to ignore his ranting. I continued running scenarios of how to respond to Neal's inquisition, and then I thought back to Ra'mon's comment about not allowing people to have too much control of my life. I continued shrugging and shaking my head as I scraped my nail against the cherry wood table in front of me.

Chace leaned over in my direction. "Dude, don't be like this. Just give him an answer?"

"Okay." *I'll give him an answer,* I thought to myself. *Hell, I'll give them all an answer.* "I don't need rehab; I don't have a problem with the drugs or alcohol. I'm just pissed that even though you and your organization say that you are all okay with my homosexuality—you're really not. I feel so trapped. I'm trapped between what you want me to be and what I am."

Directing my anger at Neal, I vented on, "I also hate that everyone feels the need to make snide comments about me and my sexuality and where I put my dick, so I just drank more out of frustration and maybe over did it on the pills," I continued. "I feel alone and I'm not happy. Period."

The room fell silent. I just knew that I was

going to be released from my contract.

Neal leaned back in his chair, absorbing all the things I had said. I think he realized that he was just as guilty by making derogatory statements to me and allowing the other members of the team to make and had not handled the situation better.

"Why didn't you just come to me? We could have discussed this matter privately," he said as he fired up a cigar.

"That's the problem. I'm tired of hiding. I would love to be open and be me. I feel so much pressure to be perfect white pop star when I'm not. It's infuriating."

"Okay, this is what we're gonna to do. I'll let you be free to speak out about your sexual orientation if you want. I will let you determine what you would or would not like to share with the public."

Dan, Neal's right hand man, made a suggestion of making my outing more official.
"Shows would pay good money for your story. We have been getting calls from everyone wanting to know more about you, and now we can give them this—you coming out—I mean, if that's the direction you'd like to go."

Neal shot a glance at my publicist and then went around the room addressing other issues that my band mates had. He also wanted to discuss my alleged "relationship" with Tiffy Stone. Thirty minutes later, Neal took a deep breath and began to rub his temples as if the next question he needed to ask pained him.

"Okay, the next topic; this Tiffy situation." I

lowered my head knowing the question that this question would be directed toward me would change the dynamic of the group and its image...if true. "Elesin, I have always told you that I didn't care where you put your dick, but shit... I'm not saying that I believe the rumors one way or another but, eventually...a statement will be needed by both camps."

I could feel the eyes boring holes into my body. The looks of suspicion, the looks of betrayal...I could just vomit. For that sake of the group and Tiffy, I lied.

"We're like brothers and I love you all. You that. You all know that I could never...let's move on."

The silence was deafening as Neal paused, then continued on.

"I mean hell, rumors can be great for sales, but I don't want tension on the stage. Elesin, you don't have to share the details now, but if there is any truth to these – rumors," he closed his eyes and opened them into the direction of MJ who was stone-faced. "For the sake of the group, this needs to be resolved by tomorrow."

By the end of the meeting, instead of releasing me from my contract Neal apologized. He also added that if anyone in our camp made me uncomfortable that I should let him know because my antics would no longer be tolerated. Neal and the management team just saw dollar signs, a new marketable demographic. If I came out publicly, it would simply create an opportunity to market to a new demographic.

The fact that we were getting massive exposure with the press and still making tons of money was not lost on them. What I had done, my onstage collapse incident, was quickly forgiven since it was proven to be dehydration.

After all, you cannot get rid of someone after revealing their sexuality. That would kick up a global firestorm of unwanted press and negative press was unwelcome by all parties. Diane was already formulating her plan of attack. Dan, Neal's right hand man, made a suggestion of making my outing more official.

Riding on an emotional high, I went to the pool area bar. Yes, if there was a bar, I was so there. I had a lot to think about and take in from our meeting. All the guys seemed cool with everything, but MJ said nothing and now, he was staring a hole in my head from across the other side of the pool. I tried not to make eye contact, but he walked over to me anyway. *Great!*

"I need to know. Did you sleep with her?" MJ asked, as he peered at me. He was also fidgeting with his hands, so I knew he was uncomfortable with confronting me. "Please, just tell me. As a friend, your friend, I deserve to know." I said nothing. I grabbed my long island iced tea and walked away. But MJ followed me toward the elevators. "Don't do this, man," he said. "Don't walk away from me."

"Would it change anything if I admit it?"

MJ looked me in the eyes with disdain but was unable to respond. How could I tell him that on a few drunken occasions of partying and one fight too many between the two of them made for, well, an interesting evening? Tiffy was just a scorned woman who used me to get back at her man for his infidelity. And since I'd always been free with my sexual encounters, never discounting anyone, I let her use me. I love women. They are all so pretty, soft and sensual.

As we waited for the elevator, I took a sip of my drink and said, "If I admitted to you that she found out about you and the LSU student you hooked up with and wanted to get back at you, would that change how you felt about me or her? Would you still be my brother?"

MJ's jaw dropped.

"Is that what you're saying? That she slept with you to get back at me?"

"Maybe," I hesitated.

"But you're gay. Why would you do that? What's your excuse for doing that to me?"

"I don't have a good answer for that? I don't know why I do some of the things I do. I don't even know how I get into some of the situations that I get into," I confessed.

MJ shook his head and then stopped and stared at me like he realized something. "You know, Tiffy and I haven't slept with each other in like four months." I shrugged my shoulders, puzzled by his revelation. Why was he telling me this? "We were more like good friends instead of boyfriend and girlfriend."

"Okay, man, where are you going with this? What does that have to do with anything?" I asked impatiently.

"Man, Tiffy is two months pregnant. And I know for a fact that it's not mine, but she won't tell me who the father is. But now I know it's yours." Unable to process what MJ said, I stood there, staring at him with a look of bewilderment.

"What...what do you mean it's mine?" I exclaimed in shock that the rumors about America's sweetheart being pregnant were true. Not only were the rumors true but I was going to be a father ....again.

"Oh, don't play dumb. You knew. But what you probably didn't know if that she's going to keep the baby against the advice of her management team. This shit could ruin her image. It could ruin her. And it's all your fault." MJ scolded. I downed the rest of my drink. MJ was fuming mad. I sighed loudly as I thought about the repercussions I was going to face once Richard found out.

"I'm sorry. I fucked up," I whispered. I turned and walked away from MJ and entered the hotel and made my way towards the elevator as the doors opened. We stepped in and just as the doors closed, MJ threw a punch that knocked me off balance. I tried to swing at him, which infuriated him even more and we had a knock down drag out in the elevator.

I was still in a half crouched position as I attempted unsuccessfully to block his blows. I could taste the blood from my busted lip as I fell to the floor pulling MJ down with me. "MJ, please!" I screamed as he slapped my face with such force that my head hit side of the elevator wall.

"Why did you have to fuck her? I loved

her," he screamed as he kicked the right side of my ribs as I tried to get up. It seemed like we were on the elevator forever. It was like being trapped in a cage with a wild animal.

Finally making it to the top floor, I lunged at MJ as the doors opened with us falling out onto the floor. Zack was roaming the halls when he heard the commotion. He came running to pull us apart and struggled to get between us.

"You two stop it. What the fuck?" he yelled.

"This bastard knocked up my girlfriend. Sorry, ex-girlfriend," MJ screamed.

I was pacing the floor, trying to compose myself and wrap my head around the confirmation of Tiffy's pregnancy and the baby's paternity.

"Shit!" I exclaimed!

"You got Tiffy pregnant?" Zack asked. "Aren't you a fucking fag? Why are you sleeping with all these fucking chicks, you selfish prick?"

I proceeded to walk away. Zack grabbed my arm and I snatched it away. "Fuck off! I don't need this right now. I was just fucking attacked in a fucking elevator by someone who is supposed to be my brother."

"You say that we're like your brothers but what kind of brother does that shit, you asshole?" Zack shouted back. He was right. I worked hard trying to be a part of this crew and now I had pissed all over it.

I turned to MJ, wiping at my bleeding lip. "I'm so sorry. I was wrong. I didn't mean to do that to you," I pleaded. "Please, forgive me."

"Right! Forgive you? Forgive this, you cock

sucking bitch!" MJ lunged at me with wild fury. I barely managed to dodge his blow. Zack grabbed him and held him at bay. "Man, it's not worth it. He's not worth it."

"I wonder how Richard would feel if he found out?" MJ threatened with his cell phone in hand.

"Please don't."

"He's going to find out anyways," he muttered through clenched teeth. MJ walked away mumbling under his breath.

After the situation calmed, Zack of course told the rest of the crew who quickly made a beeline for my room to talk and settle things.

I wasn't in the mood, but Chace, always the peacemaker, said, "Dude, we can't perform with MJ and Elesin at each other's throats. You guys have to fix this crap." Two or three drinks later, MJ and I were forced to sit at the bar to discuss our situation to keep the peace within the group.

Mellowed by the beers and cocktails, we talked about our future with the band, then discussed how we could overcome this obstacle and rebuild our friendship. It was not going to be an easy feat, but like Chace said, it needed to be done.

Chapter 10
Chance Encounters

My band mates and I stayed up for hours discussing the role I had in destroying not only the trust of my fellow band mates but how we were to maintain a working relationship. For the sake of the group's business, it was agreed that for both on and off air appearances we were only going to put on a faux supportive front.

The next day, after we met with Neal in one of the conference rooms of the hotel we were staying in. We advised him how we were going to continue to work on repairing out relationship and not jeopardize everything we've worked hard to build. Neal nodded and asked to speak with me alone about the details of my relationship with Tiffy.

"Tiffy and I are very close friends. That's all." I continued to explain. "It wasn't my intention to hurt anyone or break up MJ and Tiffy's relationship. It just happened."

Neal snorted and turned his gaze out the huge picture window to his left. As I finished what I had to say, he shared his idea on how what his plan to smooth out the information that was going to the press with his management team. "Okay. This is what we are going to do. We are going to come out with a story that that MJ and Tiffy had already broken up before you two hooked

111

up." Neal stood up and made his way over to me and sat on the corner of the mahogany table and continued on, "We won't give any specific details but we will urge the press to respect your privacy in dealing with this delicate matter."

I agreed to keep certain details quiet as the rumors defused. Diane already had her game plan and was ready to release the story to the press. Within two weeks the scandalous relationship and baby news took a back seat to the story to an A-list star found drugged out of his mind with an under-aged hooker.

We had a few days to kill before heading off to our next set of tours. Chace and I had decided to go see a musical. I know, right? Anyway, it was an interesting spin on a classic movie. I guess you could say that it was a kind of a prequel to the movie. After the show, the director invited us back stage to meet the cast, all of which were awesome.

One in particular, Mitchel Durand, caught my eye.

He was this slender six feet one, beautiful young man with striking blue eyes. He had an amazing voice and a great energy about him. I felt drawn to him and couldn't stop staring. I also could not shake the feeling that we had met before. When we were formally introduced, I extended my hand to shake his, but I think that I made him uncomfortable You know that awkward handshake that lasts way too long? That was me. I eventually let go of his hand and he was really nice about it, never quite taking his eyes off of me.

I made my way through the cast, chatting

with the cast members and ensemble. I was playing around with the props when I felt a light brush on my lower back. It was Mitchel.

"Excuse me," he smiled. "We're having a get together at my studio. It's just a few cast members and all of Hollyweird. Would you guys like to come?" He asked as I looked over to Chace who was chatting it up with some of the female cast members.

"Hey Chace!" I yelled. "Wanna go to a party after we leave here?"

"Hells yeah!" he shouted back.

"Well, I guess we're in," I answered. Mitchel asked me to stay put while he changed out of his show clothes. Naturally, I couldn't stay still, even if a gun were to my head. I roamed the halls, bumping into fans and signing a few autographs as I waited for Mitchel to change. Personally, I thought he already looked great.

I slipped outside to get some fresh air. I lit a cigarette and closed my eyes, enjoying the moment.

"I thought you left?" Mitchel said from behind me.

"No. Sorry. I needed a smoke," I said as I offered him a drag. He took the cigarette from my fingers, keeping his eyes trained on mine the whole time.

"Thanks. I needed that," he said.

"So how long have you been a part of this ensemble?"

"Umm, just about two years."

"Oh yeah? I'm assuming that you like what you do? I mean, your voice is incredible and your look...well, let's just say it would take you farther than the theater."

He shrugged. "I mean, it's okay, but I think that I'm getting a bit bored with it. When I was younger I always wanted to do musical theater, but it's not exactly what I want to do forever, ya know? I think I want to be a singer and branch out from the confines of theater work."

Chace walked out the door with one of the make-up people.

"Dude, I've been looking all over for you. I'm riding to the party with Lydia here. Did you want to ride with?" he asked.

"Nah, I've got my car."

"See ya there. Peace out!" Chace walked off throwing the peace sign in our direction with raised eyebrows. He could always tell when I was interested in someone. But, it wasn't as if I kept my feelings hidden.

Mitchel was sexy as hell. He had jet black hair, was tall and absolutely beautiful. He also had amazing style as he enhanced his beautiful blues with tons of liner. I loved those fucking glam boys.

The same way I was taking in Mitchel, he was checking me out too. I'm sure he was trying to figure me out. He had that same puzzled look on his face that most people had when they've met me. The questions were in their eyes. Is he gay? Is he bi? Is he European? Where exactly is he from?

As far as my sexuality goes, I have never hidden my attraction to both sexes. I just never made my declaration to the masses. People just assumed that I was straight but eccentric since I was married with two children. Our marriage was never what you would call traditional. The kids both lived with Jaelyn in Texas, which came in handy since I was in a shitty relationship with Richard. Let's face it. Richard was fourteen years older than me and was very temperamental but was still thought of as a longtime friend, a financial adviser and roommate.

People are just so blind and take everything at face value. If you tell them that you are a twenty-three year old, brown hair, green-eyed Caucasian who loves women, that is all the public will see. I wonder what they would say if they knew that I was biracial, only twenty-years-old and took it up the ass."

As Mitchel and I walked over to the parking lot, I asked, "
Do you want me to drive? I have a driver."

"Of course you do." He laughed and that made me chuckle a bit. My driver picked us up around the corner as we continued talking about our career choices and fashion. Once in the car, Mitchel instructed the driver on where to go. Then we got settled and had a few drinks in the car. As we sipped on our beverages, I could not keep from staring at those lips...his eyes...his--damn! *He's sexy as hell and he knows it.*

The car stopped at this complex in a questionable part of town. I told the driver that I'd be awhile and would find other transportation if needed.

"So this is where you live?" I asked as we took the elevator up to a loft.

"Yeah, me and my roommates, Daria, a

115

make-up artist, and Andre, a wannabe fashion designer." As the elevator continued to the top floor, I just could not help fantasizing about ripping his clothes off with my teeth and tying his hands up with his tight v-neck shirt.

"Here we are," he smiled as the doors opened to a flood of loud music and people dancing in the breezeway. "Welcome to mi casa!" He said as he swayed himself into the opened loft. The room was filled with plumes of smoke, some legal and some not. I trailed close behind Mitchel as he made his presence known.

"I is here! Let's get this mutha fuckin' party started!" The crowd hooted and cheered with celebratory drunkenness. I just smiled and held on tight to Mitchel's hand as he led us to the rooftop.

"Wow, this is different!" I said, taken aback by the surroundings.

"Yeah, I wanted a more psychedelic vibe." He pointed over to the corner. "There's a hookah section and other herbal smoke choices over there." He winked. "You want a drink? I need a drank fo sho."

"Yeah, I'll have a shot of something."

"Oh really. Well follow me, kind sir, to the bar."

The scene was something out of a bad '60s or '70s themed movie. Flashing colorful lights filled the rooms. Beads hung from every doorway. Then the rooftop...bean bag chairs to fuzzy loungers. It was pretty gross, but after about three or four shots, it was magical.

We had found an unoccupied section where

we could sit and talk. Mitchel and his roommates went all out on this party.

"Oh wow, I did not notice the palm reader over there," I said. I just about died from the shocked and amazement of the elaborate scene. "Seriously?"

"Yep! Believe it or not, he's actually pretty good." Mitchel chuckled while drinking his cosmo. "You should get your palm read."

"No, I'll pass."

"What? Are you a scared of the future?"

Shaking my head and rolling my eyes, I gave in. "Fine. I'll get my palm read." The whole palm reading thing wasn't ever my cup of tea. To me, it's all fake but, for entertainment sake, and for Mitchel, I'd play along. Mitchel led me to his friend Lady Lexy. She was a pre op tranny who claimed to see into the future. Her hair was in a loose updo with a few tendrils hanging.

Sitting down in front of her, she asked, "Do you want a card reading or your palm?"

"Whatever. I don't care."

"Give me your hand," she said in a deep, almost scary voice. "Ah, you've had a lot of bad things in your life." *Blah, blah, blah.* It sounded so typical and scripted. "Someone from your past is about to come back into your life," she continued. "He will be your true love. Don't push him away. This person will help you when you most need it. You are about to face an obstacle that you will not be able to handle alone. The relationship you are currently in is not good for you and it's going to get worse."

117

Then she stopped looking at my palm and said the weirdest thing that caught me completely off guard.

"Whenever you do leave him, don't go back to the house alone."

"What the fuck does that mean?" I laughed.

She leaned in close to me and whispered, "It means that once you break up with your boyfriend, stay far away from him and get more security if you have to."

The skeptic in me asked, "Okay, so can you tell me this person's name?"

"Looks like it starts with an R. Uh, Robert. Wait, no Richard."

"Fuck me! How the fuck did you know his name?" Everyone around us was just as shocked as me. So now I was even more afraid of what could come.

"Just be careful." She said as I got up from the table. I needed to refill my drink. Not only did this psychic seem to know a lot about me, but she also knew that Richard was no good for me. Damn it. She even called him out by fucking name.

Chace made his way up to the rooftop with two girls in tow.

"Hey man, you made it! I am having the best time fucking time ever," he announced louder than necessary.

"I can see that. What have you taken? Your eyes are like olive pits."

"Dude, who knows? But in the great words of the Beatles, 'I get high with a little help from my friends!'" We sat and visited with other guest, talking about projects being worked on. Future plans, aspirations, then it gravitated towards the band; tour dates and crazy fan tales. As the cups got refilled and pills got passed out, the stories kept going. Hours passed and the party began winding down. I stood over the railing to view the beautiful city lights. Then over to my right was an even better view.

"So, do you have many soirees like these often?" I asked Mitchel.

"Not really, my roommates and I got bored and decided that we needed to expand our friend base and put up a flier," he lied. "No, it's actually my roommate Daria's birthday."

"Oh, well, I must wish her a happy birthday."

"You must," he added as he sipped his drink. His eyes remained fixated on me. "I see that you wear a ring?"

"Well, I am kind of married." I shrugged.

" You're kind of married? What the hell does that mean?" he asked with raised eyebrows. "Is that your way of saying that you are separated, uh, divorced?"

"Not exactly," I tilted my head. Now Mitchel was even more confused than ever. I did not know quite how to explain that I was currently living with my longtime boyfriend, but then cheated with the nanny, began a relationship with her who eventually gave birth to my son Jerrod and later became the legal guardian to my daughter Lynnea. All I could tell Mitchel was that "It's complicated."

Chace, who was eavesdropping, just laughed

hysterically. "Believe him, it's actually really complicated." Chace got up and patted me on my shoulder. "Best of luck with this situation," he ended as he danced back to the loft. I just bit the bottom of my lip, raised two fingers and waved him off. Looking back at Mitchel, I noticed that his face had changed. His expression, blank; his interest...gone. *Dammit*!

"Well, maybe you'll explain it to me sometime," He rubbed my arm. "Tonight is all about getting our drank on. Cheers!" He raised his glass and I did the same. He walked me back into the loft and to a quieter place in the loft—his bedroom. "I still cannot figure you out. I am usually able to figure people out but not you. There is something about you that is just, well off."

"Off? Like how?"

"Well the way you talk. You go in an out of an accent that I can't quite place. Sort of Caribbean or Cajun...who knows. Then your whole look. The only thing that I am sure about is that you are a natural blonde and you are totally gay because you are too damn sexy to be straight."

"Wow, you got that much? Wait! How did you know that I was a blonde?" I asked, wondering if I had met him somewhere.

"Well, darlin', I have eyes and I've seen some of your ads with the uh, revealing publications. And we've actually worked together before."

"Really? We have?"

"Yeah, we did a shoot together a few years back. My hair was strawberry blonde then," he recalled, jarring my memory of the very sexually explicit photo shoot in Germany we had done together. The ad was to promote contraceptives. Very '90s and very provocative. It had been me, Mitchel and some chick. It was like a threesome.

"Wow, was that you? Didn't we date for a minute?"

"Yes, and you broke my heart in a million pieces."

Mitchel and I had a two-week relationship while working in Germany before getting signed with N'Step. He looked so different with his dark hair.

"I did no such thing."

I remember I was the second guy he had ever been with. I really enjoyed his company, but once the job was over, it was back to my life with Richard. "Yes, you did. Plus you were always so mysterious, like you were in hiding or something. Maybe now you can tell me more about yourself.

Mitchel continued on with trying to get insight into who I was.

"Where are you from? Oh wait, are you a foreign spy who uses the boy band gig as a ploy obtain secret U.S. government information?" We both laughed hysterically.

"What the fuck are you on?" I asked.

Mitchel shrugged and asked, "Well, give me something. I mean, are you at least American? I think you owe me at least that much since you crushed my self esteem."

"Come on. I never crushed your self esteem." Before he could beg to differ, I confessed.

"And no, I'm not American. I was actually born in Montreal, Canada but my family is from the Republic of Mauritius, east of Madagascar, Africa. The accent is French. I am also not white. Biracial—black mother, white father..."

"Really?"

"Yes, really. "

"Wow, I didn't expect that. Wait! You're half black? I would have pegged you for at least, somewhere, I don't know where actually." He laughed. "I love it though, your accent too."

"Is that all you love about me?" I flirted.

"Well, that's for another time."

"You're weird."

"I'm weird? Whatev! You're the one fucking faking American."

"I know. It's all about marketing. I just got a speech coach to learn to soften my accent for show, and gave the illusion that I was a part of this great American boy band."

"That's the fucking American way. Cheers to that!" Mitchel wiggled to the song that began playing in the background. "You should be real. The accent, I mean, it suits you."

Mitchel suddenly grabbed my arm and pulled me up to dance. We danced close with drinks in hand. As we made our way back to the living area, we continued to dance and get our drink on.

I could feel my face getting red. "I think that I need a refill." We both headed to replenish our drinks. At the bar we chatted with everyone and anyone who approached. Sharing all about the group and upcoming projects that were pending.

His roommate Daria walked over and said,"You know my friend has this mag and I swear to God that you two were in the layouts."

"Yeah, we did do a shoot together. I can't believe that you have it."

"Of course, I've got it." She explained to the group what the picture was. "It was you, Mitchel and some chick. It was like a threesome make out session. Very sexy," she added.

Mitchel nearly choked on his beverage. "Oh my God. You must get those photos.
You know what? That was hot. We so hooked up after." We both laughed at the sudden flash of the night after the photo shoot. It was in the most questionable parts of Germany. Lots of dark places, lots of crime.

I had done a whole spread in this magazine called LURE. It was an underground publication that included bands, singers and other talents in the gay community. It also showcased community events and important news stories. However, the magazine had a poor reputation of promoting sex and bad club behavior. In a nutshell, it was a soft porn magazine.

We toasted at the memory and fun times to come. The night soon came to an end. Most of the guest were gone when Mitchel walked me to the door.

"Thanks for coming out."

"Well, thank you for inviting me. So, when are we going out?"

He smiled and shook his head. "Really? You're so sure that I would ever go out with you.

That confident?"

"I am. Besides! You haven't taken your eyes off of me since we've meet."

"Well, I cannot deny my attraction for you. I mean hello, you've only been on the sexiest men's list for like four years straight," Mitchel gushed. We both laughed and just then my phone rang. It was my agent reminding me not to party too hard and get to bed. "You have two photo shoots to do in the morning and a radio interview." I had to reassure her that I would make the shoot and not to worry.

As Mitchel said his goodbyes to the last of the guests, he grabbed my arm and led me to the sofa.

"I think that I am getting way too old to party like this," he yawned.

"Yeah right!" I said. Thinking about my life and how I lived it. I should be tired. Mitchel propped his leg onto mine. "So, you have a busy day tomorrow? Well, today?"

"Yeah, two shoots and a radio interview bright and early," I said. "So I can't stay too much longer."

"I don't want you to go," he yawned. "You can stay over and we can talk some more."

"We can do that some other time, maybe later today. That is, if you're up to it." Getting up from the sofa, Mitchel pouted his bottom lip and gave in. We exchanged contact information and said our goodbyes.

"Later," I said, leaning in to kiss him on the cheek. " I really enjoyed myself and you can call me anytime."

"Will do."

Chace was long gone and probably with someone. Looking at my platinum Rolex, it was three o'clock. I wouldn't be getting much sleep since my first shoot was at nine. As I walked to a nearby coffee shop, I thought *why must I do this to myself? Depriving myself of sleep and running on fumes? Oh the life of a pop star/model. Well, I still have some magic powder to get me through the day.*

The ringing of my phone woke me up. *Where the hell is it?* I thought as I searched around in unfamiliar territory. *Where am I?* Ah! Buried underneath my jeans, which were on the floor, was my BlackBerry.

"Hello?" I quickly answered before the call went to voicemail.

"Where are you, Ales?" Dehlia yelled. My sister was now interning at Blaze as the assistant to my agent Diane. I hated when she called me by my middle name, it made me feel like a small child.

"Oh, shit! What time is it?"

"It's 8:30!" she screamed. "You were supposed to be at the office at eight. Where are you? I'll send the car."

"No, I know where I'm going. I'll be there," I reassured and ended the call. *Where the hell am I? Shit! I must have drifted off…somewhere…with someone?* I checked myself I looked down to check the goods.

A male voice from the door spoke. "You're up."

"Who the fuck are you?" I asked, still in a drunken haze.

"I'm the man you fucked this morning," he answered. "Would you like some coffee?"

"Yes, sorry!" I apologized. "Where am I exactly?" I asked, confused by my apparent drug-induced amnesia.

"That's okay." He handed me a cup of hot java. "There you go, sweetie," the gorgeous stranger said.

"Where exactly did we meet?" I asked, before sipping my coffee while still checking around for my clothing.

"Well, first off, I'm Juda. And we met at the coffee shop down the street," he answered. "You looked like you were waiting on someone."

Apparently, I got bored waiting on my driver to find me and went home with this cute, five-nine tanned hot body. Even in a drunken stupor, I still knew how to pick'em.

"I'm a huge fan of your music, and an even bigger fan of your...body of work," he said looking me up and down.

I really need to slow down on my substance intake. "Yeah, thank you. I appreciate that."

"I guess that little pill I gave you counter acted whatever you took before," he confessed.

Just then my phone chimed, and I answered quickly.

"If you are not at this shoot in the next fifteen minutes, your ass is grass buddy!" Dehlia screeched then hung up. All I could do was down my coffee and ask Juda for a quick shower.

As the steamy hot water beat down on my head, a moment of clarity filled my mind. This was typical Elesin fashion. In less than five hours I'd hooked up with a fan and forgotten the whole thing. I guess my body just crashed.

I heard a knock on the door. It was Juda.

"You need me to help wash your back?" he smiled as he stepped into the shower with me.

Damn! What was I supposed to do? At least this time I'd remember. I sure loved those dark haired, Latin guys.

I grabbed his ass with both hands—nice and tight. Shoving my tongue down his throat, he moaned in ecstasy. I forced him around and pushed him against the wall. Then I shoved every ounce of my nine and a half inch cock up his ass. He screamed with pleasure. At least this time I would not forget, and neither would he.

Chapter 11
Business as Usual

Juda was really sweet to drive me to my destination. Fortunately, I was not too far from the shoot location, but I was still fashionably late. My first meeting with this particular photographer and my first impression was going to be a diva move. Whatev!

Dehlia, was waiting in the back when we pulled up. She looked so different. Her hair was dark brown, straightened and cut in an asymmetrical bob. Any familial resemblance that we may have had was long gone. She looked more like a legal aid than a marketing agent with a navy blue skirt suit and matching heels. She was so upset with my tardiness that she did not say a word to me. I just followed her into the building and was whisked right to hair and makeup. Dehlia finally calmed down to scold me. "What's your excuse this time? Who was that guy that dropped you off?"

"Trust me, you don't wanna know."

She rolled her eyes and led me to the cold studio. It was way too cold for what I was shooting for, a jean ad, which meant I was shirtless and sporting low rise jeans that came down just enough to see the top of my ass.

The photographer wanted a lot of profile shots, me leaning back, pelvis up and chest and

128

arms glistening under the lights. Most of the shots were very suggestive. We did about six different looks and about ten different styles of jeans.

Three hours later, I was on my way to another shoot. This one was going to be more glam rock, with me wearing thick black eye liner, gloss for the lips and the tightest pants I could barely walk in. Fortunately, the radio interview was via telephone, so I could go back to my hotel room at the Hilton, order room service and relax.

By 5:00 I was getting my bath ready. I called in to the station at 6:15. I did the whole interview while chilling out in the jetted tub. DJ·Q did a brief intro and started right in asking questions about my personal life rather than the charity event I would be attending with the band.

"Now, there were some pictures circulating on the Internet of you with your tongue down a few men's throats back in the day. There were also loads of pictures of you in drag. Did you ever officially come out of the closet?" he asked.

"Well, I didn't realize that I needed to. I don't care to comment on the lip locking, cross dressing photographs. That's old news, man."

DJ Q interrupted. "Why don't you just set the record straight? Are you straight, gay, or bi?" He continued. "The public wants to know, especially after you were rumored to have gotten Tiffy Stone pregnant."

"I mean, it is what it is. I like to play dress-up. If that includes me in drag, I'm all for it. I have gone to a lot of clubs and parties with many cocktails…and things happen," I answered. "People see what they want to see. It's all an illusion. What I project has nothing to do with sexuality. As far as Tiffy goes, that's a personal matter that I am not comfortable talking about."

"Okay, so what is it that you are trying to project?" he asked.

"It depends on how I feel. If I feel like rocking it out, I'll add a bit of eye liner, maybe some glitter. If I want to be more casual and project a more approachable, guy-next-door type, I'll put on some jeans and a polo shirt."

"So, what's the act or illusion?" he asked. "Are you gay and going through the motions of portraying a straight man?"

"No, not at all. I am as real as they come. People are too consumed with labels instead of focusing on what's important, like the reason I called the show."

DJ Q was not giving up. He screeched, "We'll get to the charity event later. Let's just clear the air and settle the rumors once and for all. Are you gay?" He paused. "Yes or no?"

"How about this? My heart could belong to a man or a woman." I answered. "Especially when it comes to the hearts of the children, men and women who will be receiving assistance with their cancer treatments…" I continued on with what the organization was about and how the public could participate in donating their time and money.

"Aw man! You're just gay!" he shouted.

"Why are you so adamant that I proclaim that I'm gay? Are you interested or something?" I giggled. "Would it change how you feel about me?"

"No, we still love you and your little gay boy band." DJ Q chuckled. "Okay, okay , now we can get back to why you called." DJ Q wavered. He finally spent time promoting the charity, Hope for Angels.

The interview didn't start the way I expected, but I think I added more mystery to my persona. I find it quite funny how before fame and money— well, I've always had money; the fame is a new one for me—no one cared who I was, what I did or who I'd done. I am just surprised that no one had dug further into my past life, my life before N'Step. When they did...they found my estranged mother and step-father lounging and living a quiet life in Baton Rougue, Louisiana.

What I was most afraid of was them finding out I was abused and had a mother who did not help me, did not save me from the man who not only raped me daily but tortured me as well.

When I think about the video of me being sexed by various men, I just could not bear having that come out and having to face my children. Although, it would certainly be a slap in the face to my mother who never believed that my uncle did the things he did to me. Hell, maybe the video should come out. How could she have not known what was happening to me? She walked in on us that day she... fucking bitch! I hate her so much for what she allowed my uncle to do to me. But I can't, I need her to acknowledge me.

Sitting on the balcony, smoking a joint, and drinking some Jack, I contemplated what I should do for the night. Sleep, party or sleep? I decided the latter. I needed to relax and get some rest. Then the phone rang.

It was Mitchel. "You got any plans for this evening?"

"Nothing planned. Just hanging out in my room then probably going to bed with you on my mind," I said.

"Aw! I knew you couldn't get me out of your head. The plan worked." He laughed menacingly. I could not help laughing as well. "So, you want any company?"

"Yes, of course. That would be nice." I gave him the location of the Hilton and ended the call. I walked over to the door to leave it slightly ajar and went back to the balcony and waited for him to arrive.

Thirty minutes later, he pushed open the door and found me out on the balcony. "Hey you," he smiled. I rose from my seat to greet him with a welcoming hug. He smelled so good.

"So how was your day? Planning any more parties?" I asked.

He giggled as he sat down on the available chair.

"No. Not this week--"

"Oh, where are my manners? Want anything to drink, smoke or… other?" I winked.

"I could do a drink. What'cha got?"

"Everything."

As I fixed Mitchel a drink, he threw a question at me that I guess had been nagging at him since the night before.

"So, are you going to explain to me your current living situation and marriage?"

"What do you want to know?"

"You told me that you were in a long-term relationship with some man but married to the mother of your children."

Mitchel sat there listening intensely to an abbreviated tale of my life. I explained how at fifteen I ran away with Lynnea and Richard my boyfriend of two years, then hired a nanny, Jaelyn, who I had an affair with. The end result was my son Jerrod. I married Jaelyn to help keep my children away from my volatile relationship with Richard.

Mitchel's eyes were wide as saucers as I talked about my relationship with Jaelyn.

"You must really lover her? I mean—it's understandable but?" Mitchel interrupted.

"But what?" I asked as Mitchel began to shift uncomfortable in the chair.

"But – where does that leave you with potential lovers?"

That question caught me a bit by surprise as I sat there staring at someone I could see myself being with. He was tall, talented and smart beyond belief but I knew that starting up a relationship with him would be disastrous to say the least.

"Ideally, I would love to be in one uncomplicated relationship. And who knows – for the right person, I could see myself giving it all up for him."

Mitchel's perfectly arched eyebrow rose but he maintained his smirk as I continued on, "Right now, I just need a friend more than anything."

"So, that's it?" he asked. "That's pretty complicated. I am assuming that you and Richard have a sort of open relationship."

"Sort of. He understands that I am on the road most of the time touring. And there are a lot of temptations out there. His only rule is to not begin a relationship with somebody else."

"Do you love him?

"Sometimes." I quickly changed the subject to find out more about this gorgeous blued-eyed man on my balcony. "Let's talk about you."

"Oh, oh! What do you want to know?" He shifted in his chair and took another huge gulp out of his cup.

"I know you were a model. I know that you are into musical theater but tell me more about yourself?"

He shared details of his upbringing in the Northeast. He had a two parent household with a younger brother who loved him and were supportive of everything he did. Even when he came out to them, they were right by his side.

I was envious of the relationship that he had with his family. It was something that I've always wanted and tried to create with my own.

He continued on as I questioned him about his career and what he wanted to do when he grew up. He laughed.

"Well, I'd love to be a fairy princess." He fluttered his hands out to his sides as if they were wings.

I rolled my eyes in response.

"Nah, I want to be a professional singer,

not necessarily a famous singer but that's my passion."

"You can do it. I can see that fire in your eyes. You want it bad don't you?"

"You have no idea—of how bad…I want it," he enunciated each and every syllable. He leaned over towards me and puffed out his gorgeous bottom lip and continued, "And if that doesn't work then I need to get a set up like Jaelyn and be a housewife, Mitchel chuckled.

"Well for that, you would have to bare my child."

"Oh, bitch don't think that I couldn't find a baby somewhere," he retorted. We laughed uncontrollably. Maybe it was the alcohol, maybe the pot, but we could not stop laughing.

Somehow our conversation turned into a more serious topic. I shared with him some of the neglect that I experienced as a child. I even sharing with Mitchel that I had thoughts about killing myself on many occasions. I omitted the sexual abuse and how I almost killed-- Well, it was not a great time for me. Talking to Mitchel made me think about my past, remembering my birthdays, which were especially harsh. Come to think of it, I don't have one pleasant memory from my childhood.

Suddenly feeling weary, I yawned and stretched my arms to the sky. "I am so tired."
Mitchel rose out of his chair and walked over to me. He ran his fingers through my hair.

"Let's go to bed then." He took my hand in his and led me to the bed.

Seductively, he removed my clothing; first

the shirt, then the pants. He rose up slowly, with his lips running up my abs...my chest...my neck. His kisses were so sweet. His lip gloss, cherry flavored. He tasted so good. He quickly removed his own clothes and we explored each other's bodies, teasing and sucking anything and everything.

"Fuck me!" Mitchel groaned. "Fuck me now." He pulled my hair and bit my neck. We fucked like insatiable teenagers until we were sore.

The next morning I woke up to an empty spot on the bed. *Oh well*, I thought. I yawned and slid myself out of my bed. Feeling the need for a smoke, I went over to the balcony, and there he was, smoke in one hand and coffee in the other. His freshly washed face surprised me and "Holy shit, you are covered in freckles," I exclaimed.

"Yeah, I know. It's a rare sight," he smiled while fluttering his eyes at me.

"I like them. You look so wholesome, almost innocent."

"Right! Hard to believe that concealer and heavy eye makeup can sexy you up," he said as he flipped his hair. "So, what are the plans of the day? Any more photo shoots?"

"Nah, nothing today. I have that charity thing to do today, but that is only for two hours."

"You want go out later?"

"Yeah, that would be cool. Actually, I do have something planned for tonight, but you are free to join me."

"Oh, and what is that?"

"A friend of mine has this drag club and asked me to perform one of my routines that I did a few months back."

"In drag? Which club?"

"It's called The Underground. And yes, sometimes I do drag. But once every few months she has a showcase where the queens—or others— perform, singing live."

"Where's this?"

"On Glendale Boulevard," I continued. "Miss Sabrina Starr and her partner Hylan Parc love to put together these themed showcases for everyone to participate. During the summer, she likes to put on a concert full of theatrics and talent."

"That sounds so fun. I would love to do something like that," Mitchel said.

"You should."

"So what will you be performing? Will it be in drag?"

"No, just glammed. The theme with be glam rock. I'll be doing Bowie's Fame."

"Awesome! I would so love to see your performance in drag."

"Well, you can go online. Look up Ferocia Couture. Don't ask." I laughed. "Just look it up."

Ferocia Couture was the character I created in drunkin fun with my friends. It was given to me for my love of fashion and fearlessness.

People already suspected that I lived an alternative lifestyle, but it was neither confirmed nor denied. I mean all they had to do was search YouTube and they could pretty much have that question answered.

Mitchel and I continued to share tales of our future plans. He talked about his family. I envied his strong family support. Getting hungry we ordered breakfast and then enjoyed each other's bodies...once on the balcony and again in the shower.

"So, you said that you left home at fifteen. Have you seen anyone in your family since then?"

"Yeah, while on tour I bumped into my father. Not a very pleasant meeting," I answered.

"Well, why not?"

"Well, I think that I expected too much from him. I was hoping that he'd want to sit with me and talk to me about – well, everything. Unfortunately, that wasn't the case; he just gave me a hug and said, 'it was really nice seeing you. I can't stay and chat, I have to get to this important meeting.'" I answered uncomfortable and began biting my lip as I remembered the encounter.

"Ouch!" Mitchel winced. "Have you seen anyone else?"

"Well my sister I see on occasion, but we're not that close but I got her a job interning at my agency."

"Well that's cool."

"Yes, if it weren't for my families dysfunction, I may not have become the person I am today."

"Good for you. You're a fucking success story. You should write a book," he suggested.

"Yeah, it would probably make the best sellers list with all the sex, violence and debauchery," I joked.

"Sex?"

"Yes, unfortunately, but that's for another day," I confessed. He was very apologetic. I assured him that I was okay and that he did not need to apologize. We winded down our conversation and made plans to meet at the club. Kissing Mitchel good-bye, I thanked him for his company. I watched as he entered the elevator. Then he was gone.

Chapter 12
New Found Friendship

Over the next few months Mitchel and I were fast becoming the best of friends and more. We shared a lot—stories, music, dreams and our passions. I could just look at Mitchel all day. His eyes were the most beautiful eyes I'd ever seen. And his pouty lips, I could just suck on those for days. Sometimes, I did.

He and I had tried to spend as much time together as we could. Between his shows and my obligations, there were times when I'd have him meet me at a location so that we could enjoy each other's company. He got a kick out of my lifestyle. To him, it was exciting, the rush of adrenaline, the screaming fans and the worldwide travel. He so wanted that "rock star" lifestyle. I warned him against it, but it never deterred him, at all.

It was nice having people in my life that I could be with that made me feel important and loved. With Richard, it felt like my love was more of an obligation. I felt real love with Christian, but that was not a reality. He wasn't ready to be out and I wasn't ready to leave Richard.

With our rapidly changing schedules, we were almost too busy to work on anything else. I guess it didn't help much that I was in a screwed up relationship and screwed anyone who showed me interest. Put in Christian's situation, I wouldn't jump into a relationship with me either. Regardless of the situation, I knew deep down, he loved me just as much as I loved him.

Christian was touring all around the world which left me alone in a miserable relationship with Richard, one that I was unsure of how to get out of. However, this alone time also brought me closer to Mitchel, who was great. He and I could go out at night and get all dressed up. We'd get in full makeup and work the club scene. When we met up in L.A. he would take me through his old stomping grounds—lots of sex, drugs and rock n' roll.

Tiring of the nightlife, Mitchel suggested that I invite him to my home. He had never seen it. Typically, I'd hang out at Mitchel's place or hotels at various locations. Guess I was always afraid that I would get caught by Richard, that he'd find me fucking some strange man in our bed. That was a no-no in our household, but that did not stop me from welcoming Mitchel into my home.

"This is a kick ass place you got here," Mitchel ogled as he made his way through the house. I gave him the grand tour of the whole mansion with its open kitchen with garden *views* and Stainless steel appliances.

He was in awe of how clean and new everything looked. He nearly fainted at the site of the huge den with the glass partition that opened up to the backyard. He was in love.

"You know you will have to kick me out. I am so not leaving here," he joked.

"Well, I guess I could explain to Richard

that you are my personal, very personal assistant," I laughed. Heading down the back stairs, we made our way to the backyard.

"You've got to be fucking kidding me! Look at this fucking pool. Gorg!" he exclaimed as he began to peel off layers of his clothing until there was nothing. I followed suit as we proceeded to jump into the pool. The view, the reason I picked this house, was absolutely amazing. The pool overlooked the Hollywood Hills which were highlighted by the sparkling lights of the stars above and from the town below. I swam over to through the waterfall grotto which included a bar area where I fixed us some of my famous martinis.

As I was shaking the cocktails, Mitchel came up from behind to kiss the nape of my neck.

"That feels so good," I exhaled as I began to rub my ass into his crotch. Feeling his excitement, he pulled my hair, yanking my head back to meet his mouth. Sticking his tongue deep inside, I moaned with pleasure. I could hardly catch my breath as he began to play with my dick, which grew with every stroke.

"Stop!" I grunted, trying not to explode right then and there. "Slow down."

I spun around and pushed Mitchel against the wall of the pool. My eyes met his gaze. Then I let my tongue explore his neck, working my way down to his nipples. He screamed with pleasure as I gently bit down and then flicked my tongue, making his eyes roll to the back of his head.

Taking both of his hands and pulling my hair back he said, "I'm going to fuck you like a porn star." I quickly propped myself up on the bar seat as Mitchel made his way between my legs. My breathing laboring as he lifted my ass up, teasing me with his cock. He rubbed around my highway to heaven until neither one of us could take it anymore and thrust himself inside of me.

His size caught me off guard as my head went back and hit the grotto wall. He didn't rush anything—just took his time until the orgasmic ripples ran throughout my body. He lifted my ass up and thrust his cock inside.

Afterwards, we made stumbled into the guest bedroom and passed out onto the bed.

Waking up the next morning in Mitchel's arms was heavenly. The sun was shining bright through the bay windows and the smell of fresh coffee being brewed permeated the air. Yummy! My housekeeper must have been downstairs. Good thing we made it to the room. Although, it wouldn't be the first time she'd seen me in various stages of...well, just various stages.

Even though Mitchel knew that I had a live-in boyfriend, it did not matter to him. He just enjoyed being with me. Unfortunately, our relationship lasted only five months before it came to an abrupt end. Following the scent to the heavenly smell of coffee, I strolled into the kitchen and was shocked to find Richard at the kitchen island, reading a paper.

"Mornin' sunshine," he said. "Want some coffee?" My heart sank into the pit of my stomach as I froze into place. He was not supposed to be back for another month.

Finally able to force a smile and respond, I walked over to him for an embrace.

"Hey baby. When did you get in?"

"Not long...but long enough to see that we have a house guest."

The forced smile upon Richard's face quickly faded into a snarl.

"How long has this been going on?" he asked as he locked me within his arms. My heart pounded against my chest so hard that I could feel it bouncing off his chest.

"Not long," I said as my eyes began to water. "He's just a friend," I answered as I tried to break free from his grips.

"Really? Just a friend?" Richards embrace feeling more like being trapped in the jaws of life. Just then, Mitchel found his way to the kitchen.

"Oh, hey. Am I interrupting something?" He asked visibly shocked at this uncomfortable scene. Richard suddenly released me, walked over to Mitchel and offered him a cup of coffee. We sat in the kitchen nook area, Richard over exaggerated his affection towards me by kissing my neck every few minutes and touching various parts of my body.

Mitchel soon excused himself to get dressed. Richard leaned in to me as I sat with a false smile on my face and fear in my eyes. He whispered, "This relationship ends today. When he leaves we're going to have a little discussion." The smile on my face slowly faded as turned my gaze towards my coffee and sulked. I knew that when Mitchel left, Richard would have me regretting my carelessness in bringing Mitchel into our home.

My shoulders crept up towards my ears with tension as I walked Mitchel to the door. I knew that as soon as the door shut behind him, Richard was going to lay into me with his fist. I began to slow my breathing, trying to keep myself calm as my head rested on the door. I jumped as Richard's hand reached out to touch my shoulder.

"It's okay. I'm not angry, just upset."

"What?" I was shocked. He's not yelling at me, he's not htting me. Who is this man? I turned to face him as he placed my face between his hands and kissed my lips tenderly.

"I love you baby, just no more. No more playing around. Be with me and only me. Can you do that for me?" His eyes welled up with tears as he placed his cheek against mine. "Will you do that for me?"

I didn't know what to say. I was so taken aback with this new side of Richard that I hadn't seen since we first met. This is the Richard that I've missed, the Richard that I fell in love with years ago. Then I closed my eyes, took in a breath and remembered...this is also the Richard that I fear. And out of fear, I answered, "Okay."

My band-mates and I were doing a bunch of shows and charity events in Tampa, Florida. I sent for Mitchel to come and hang out before he began his tour. I knew that having him meet up with me after being caught by Richard was risky but I didn't care. We got to have lunch at the Council Oak Steak & Seafood and catch a movie at the Regency 20. Once back at the hotel, we did some lines, drank and had some mind-blowing sex for the rest of the night.

We fell asleep spooning each other into the next morning. We were and awakened by a loud noise that startled us from sleep.

"Son of a whore!" Richard yelled as he smacked me in the back of the head. Mitchel and I rose clumsily in shock when we saw an irate Richard standing before us.

"Richard, what are you doing here?"

"What am I doing here? What the fuck are *you* doing here?" Richard shouted, grabbing me by the neck.

Mitchel tried to intervene.

"What the fuck, man? Stop it," he screamed as Richard turned his attention and rage towards him. Richard released his grip from my neck, and threw me down to the floor. He yanked Mitchel off the bed and drug him into the restroom and slammed the door shut. I was unable to get to Mitchel in time as my legs failed from beneath me.

I tried to beat down the door yelling at Richard to open the door. I heard Mitchel scream bloody murder. I felt helpless as I banged on the door and hollered at Richard to open the door but I got no response. All I could hear were the banging of bodies being tossed around. I could hear Mitchel crying and I cried.

Suddenly, I heard a soft thud to the floor and muffled words being said that I couldn't quite make out. I just kept beating on the door, hoping Richard would stop his rage-filled assault.

"I'm going to make you forget about

146

Elesin," I heard him say to Mitchel. Mitchel screamed and then it was quiet.

As the door opened, Richard stalked toward me, breathing heavy, with a look I'd never seen before. His eyes alternated between empty, wild and then dead.

Meanwhile Mitchel was laid out face down on the cold, marble floor bruised and raped. All I could do was cry. It was my fault. This was all...my fault. As Mitchel slowly rose from the floor, he used the back of his hand to wipe away the tears trailing down his face and the blood dripping from his nose. He limped awkwardly back into the room to retrieve his clothes.

Richard broke his gaze from me, and glared back at Mitchel. "Now when you think of Elesin, you will always see me. Now get your fucking clothes on and get the fuck outta here."

Mitchel did what he was told, clearly in shock. He said nothing to me as I stared on with apologetic eyes. Richard stood between us to ensure that I did not go to Mitchel's aid. Although I wanted to, I couldn't. Richard would kill me for sure. At that moment I knew it would be the last time that I'd ever see Mitchel again and as he left the room, I braced myself for the first blow.

When Richard was done working me over, I thought for sure that he was going to kill me. I had broken Richard's number-one rule: "Don't start a relationship with anyone." After he had come home early to surprise me, the surprise was on him when he saw Mitchel and me in the pool creating more than waves. Richard beat the shit out me once

147

Mitchel left and warned me never to see him again. I lay there broken as Richard continued his verbal attack on me, calling me worthless and ungrateful. He was right.

Fortunately, Richard left my face alone. It was my body that was in real bad shape. I had to do a show that night and every step I took was painful. I cleaned myself up after Richard calmed and tried my best to look somewhat normal. Chace knew something was wrong right away when I met up with him and rest of the group in the lobby. Once the guys found out what happened, it was all over. Jazz and Zack went up to my room to confront Richard, but he was already gone.

During our show, my energy level was low. My body ached and my heart just wasn't into it anymore. I wasn't into anything anymore. After four years in the group, I had become pretty ingenious at covering up my injuries from Richard's beat downs. But now our management team began to realize that those "accidents" and "bar fights" were all bullshit. This time, I had really screwed up. Richard was never going to be able to forgive me or trust me again. I knew that my encounter with him in the hotel room was only the beginning, my punishment was just beginning. It was like my punishment was never ending.

Richard had unleashed more anger and fury all over me and my face once I got home from the gigs. Being that Richard had the body of a prized cage fighter and the rage of a rabid dog, I could never take him. It was a lose/lose situation.

When he finally left, I called Chace. Hearing

me whimper on the other end of the phone, he rushed over and forced me to go seek medical attention. After a two-hour wait, a thorough examination and x-rays, the doctor said I had a fractured orbital bone, left wrist sprain and four bruised ribs. Naturally, he wanted to know what happened, but I remained tight-lipped. He went on and on about the importance of filing a report if I had been attacked. I just wanted my medical treatment, meds and to be home.

Chace asked the question I had asked myself so many times, "Why are you staying in this miserable relationship with that punk ass Richard?" All I could do was shrug.

Chace ended up staying with me all night. He wanted to be there for me and make sure I took my prescribed medication. I guess he fell asleep next to me in bed because when Richard returned, I heard his voice booming.

"What the fuck is this?" he yelled. "You've already got some random trick lined up. You just couldn't wait for me to leave."

"What are you talking about?" Chace quickly sat up to stand guard.

"I'm not some trick you asshole. There isn't anything going on here. You need to chill. Haven't you done enough?" Chace scolded. Richard just stood there, motionless as Chace jumped out of bed and squared his shoulders to a man who towered over him. "I'm just sayin'. You've messed him up pretty bad. You broke his fucking face and almost broke his ribs, or don't you care?"

"I'm sorry, baby," Richard said as he leaned

in to kiss my forehead. "I was just upset but I swear it will never happen again."

"Right. You've said that before," I said, just above a whisper.

"This time I mean it. I will do anything. I don't want to lose you."

"Whatever!" Chace threw his hands up in disgust.

I glared at Richard and said," You're on the couch tonight. I'm way too tired for this right now. Chace stays here." Surprisingly, he walked away quietly. Chace climbed back in bed, I took another pain pill and off to sleep we went.

Unfortunately, I was unable to make my appearance for the morning show the next day. I still had a badly beaten face that I would not be able to explain to the public. I had already been warned by management and my agent about having to miss engagements so it wasn't a surprise when a few days later, my band mates and I had to fly out for a mandatory meeting with the management team.

Most of the meeting was about me and how my personal life was interfering with the band's promotion. When one messes with the band's image, you are messing with not only the band's money but most importantly, the producers' money. That was unacceptable. I was given a final warning to straighten up and make drastic changes.

My schedule in September was going to be exhausting. We had to do some many shows, charity events, movie premiers, and photo op after photo op scheduled. The touring gave me plenty of time to think about a way to break from Richard. Every other night, I had a card and gifts from him apologizing for what he did to me. I couldn't even bare to talk to him or think about him. Every time I looked in the mirror, the reminder of his rage covered my body in healed bruises.

Once the bruising healed, I began feeling good about myself again. I was not only on time for gigs but I was often early to hair and makeup. My stylist Ra'mon would hook me up, I'd perform to perfection. We were interviewing and performing non-stop for three weeks before our three day break in Florida.

Ra'mon and I used that time to party hard, sometimes, too hard. The amount of drugs we were offered and the sex was outrageous! Life truly could not have been any better. I had no limits, no self-control and no one around to reel me back to reality. More importantly, no thought of Richard.

Although I was not publicly out yet, I had been asked by friends to make an appearance at this gay bar called The Metro. This club was one of the biggest venues in Jacksonville, Florida with its multileveled themed bars and clubs. They housed everything from a sports themed game room to a lively club with the pulsating lights and beats bouncing off the walls. Half naked boys waltzed around, gyrating and serving the patrons in their decorative tighty whities.

My band mates stressed that I needed to be especially cautious, especially safe and especially on time for the show the next day. They really had skewed views of what gay bars were about. Like most people thought of gay bars as a modern day

Sodom and Gomorrah with naked men hanging from the ceilings. Men openly having sex unprotected sex in every nook and cranny. Things like that don't really happen--except on Wednesdays.

Contrary to what people believe, gay bars are no different than what you'd see in the straight bars. We like to dance, drink and socialize like most people. The only difference is that there are half dressed men walking around servicing questionable color coded drinks to everyone and boys dancing around in cages. Besides, sex parties are typically by invitation only.

I invited Ra'mon my personal friend and stylist and a mutual friend of ours, Chris to attend the bar with me. We were going to have a blast. Once at the bar, Ra'mon was like a kid in a candy store, amongst a multitude of dancers displaying their hard, hairless, sweaty bodies.

"Boys, boys everywhere," Ra'mon sang. "Yield to me boys. Bend to my will or my massively huge dick." Ra'mon twirled around touching every chest he could.

"You are a mess," I chuckled. Ra'mon and Chris were a lot of fun but they were out there. Both of them were very flamboyant. Ra'mon looked like a cross between 1980's Prince and Jermaine Stewart--high heeled boots and all. Ra'mon at six-foot-three towered over everyone when he was in heels.

Chris on the other hand, was rail thin and short. He was a very blonde, very blue eyed, very waifish man in a twelve year old girl's body. He had more of a punk style. If it had chains, leather or some kind of metal on it--he wore it. And I am still trying to figure out how the dinner forks of the places we've dined with became his accessories shortly after.

"I need cocktail...and by cocktail. I mean a cock in my tail," Chris grumbled as he leaned himself against the bar, eyeing men from one end of the bar to the other.

"Not liking the selection?" I asked as Chris rolled his eyes at an approaching subject. Chris was could be a bit of a snob but once you get to know him, he was great. He was newly single, on the prowl but still pining away for his lost love.

"Ugh! Everyone here is so--Ug."

"Oh, come on. We are surrounding by a nice selection of men. What is with you? You have been in a bad mood since we got here."

"I have not. I just... I'm just...horny as hell and no one's talking to me." He sulked. "Damn elitist pricks." Chris stomping his feet made Ra'mon and I giggle like little school boys, ensuring not to spill our tasty beverages.

"Well, if you want, I'll take you to the back and show you a really good time," I offered. Chris was not amused. Chris continued drinking and making his way through the bar to get far away from us as possible. Chris eventually got bored and went home...alone as Ra'mon and I continued to chat with men who were not fans of my music but fans of my printed works.

There were individuals at the bar who were not fans and made it known to the whomever listened. The same men whose advances I had rejected earlier were beginning to get belligerent and disruptive. Oh I so loved the haters, talking about me being fake and hiding my homosexuality, posting that I wasn't gay enough. "Assholes!"

What more could I do aside from waving a rainbow flag everywhere I went and sing show tunes. Seriously? I hate show tunes. Get over it. I mean how many guys' dicks do I needed to suck to prove how gay I was. Fortunately, I was able to enjoy the rest of the night as I walked around looking for Ra'mon.

Giving up my search for my friend, I sat down on an unoccupied barstool and ordered another drink. Swiveling myself around I noticed a gorgeous tall, tanned, blonde haired, blue-eyed Greek god checking me out from the right side of the bar. His attire screamed frat boy. Backwards baseball cap, light blue polo shirt and tight jeans-- not that I noticed. I gave a quick smile of acknowledgment in his direction to which he reciprocated.

Making his way towards me, beer in hand to introduce himself.

"Hey! I'm Brenden."

"Elesin." Taking his extended hand into mine and proceeded to chat. As he spoke, I continued sipping on my vodka cran, unable to control the smile on my face. The only thing I could think about was how I was going to have him worshiping my dick later. Distracted by the possibilities, his words were a blur. I think he said he played at the University of Central Florida. I also

think that he mentioned that he was in a fraternity--
Sigma Alpha Epsilon. Who knows?

"Hey. There's a party at my apartment.
Would you like to come with?" He asked. He could
have asked me to place my tongue in various places
on his body and I would accept. "I'm in." I
smiled.

Finishing off the remainder of my drink and
following Brenden out of the bar and into his
mustang convertible. Driving off, with the top
down, we shared tales of crazy fan encounters. I
thought that the fans my band mates and I had were
crazy. But I think that football fanatics take the
cake. Let's just say that beer and guns don't mix.

I had noticed earlier that their weren't a lot
of girls at this thing but we did arrive to the party
late. There were a few female stragglers who
appeared too wasted to know where they were.
After awhile, Brenden and I made our way upstairs
to one of the rooms, his room. The room was
spacious, beige walls and bedding. Trophies and
ribbons along the shelves. Typical athletes bed
room, yet surprisingly clean and tidy.

I was shoved onto the bed so fast, with such
force that it caught me off guard and left me a bit
winded. Brenden began kissing me so forcefully
that I could hardly catch my breath. It was exciting.
My head was whirling and my limbs weak but I
fought against it. "Wait!" I gasped. "I don't feel so
good. I'm so dizzy."

"I know. Just relax. You'll be fine," he
reassured. Slowing down his pace, kissing my neck
then my lips. It felt so good but at the same time,

scary. I had no control of my body, my limbs felt as if I were submerged in thick mud. My breathing was quickening in both fear and pleasure.

"No. Don't." I murmured as he continued pumping himself inside me. I winced with the images of my uncle forcing himself upon me. The same words being uttered in my ear, the same words Sebastian would say. My eye lids growing heavier with every blink. When he was done, he said something to me that I couldn't quite make out. I wasn't sure what was happening to me. I attempted to gain control of my body as what seemed to be a kaleidoscope of the men having their way with me flashing in my mind. I wasn't sure if I were in a horrible dream or having a horrible trip.

I had awakened to a strange voice trying to rouse me. Once my eyes opened, I saw the same gorgeous man that I met at the bar hovering over me with a concerned look on his face. "Elesin? Elesin are you okay."

"Yes, I'm fine. What time is it?" I just could not believe that this had happened to me again. I had blacked out and found my way into a stranger's bed.

Weakened from the terrible hangover, I drug my body out of bed and looked around for my clothes.

"It's 3:45," He chimed.

"P.M.?" Shit. I've missed rehearsals. Just then, my phone began to ring as I ignored the call, I forced myself to get my clothes on and make my way the studio pronto.

Brenden stood there confused and amused

by my frantic movements. "Do you need a ride?"

"No. Just get me a cab, please." Brenden pulled out his cell phone and made a call for a cab. The shame and utter disbelief that I had found myself in this situation was unfathomable. I dreaded the thought of having to explain another missed meeting to my band mates.

My cab had arrived just as I had gotten myself together. By the time I reached my hotel, my body shook nervously as I was coming down from the drugs in my system and the chill from the fall air. Somehow, I managed to make it up to the room undetected. I struggled to hop into the shower without incident. The scorching hot water beat down on my skin as I scrubbed the pain away. I made it in time to the Jacksonville Veterans Memorial Arena to participate in the meet and greet with the fans.

As we sat and meet with our fans, Chace leaned over to me to ask, "So? What's his name?" Chace had the same look of frustration on his face that the other band-mates had displayed on their faces. When they looked at me, their distaste was covered by the faux smiles that we had to present to the fans.

"Sorry I was late. I was..."

Chace cut me off before I could explain. "No! I don't want another story as to why you look as if you just got back from a rave. I don't care. Just take some responsibility for your actions." He shook his head in disapproval. The other band mates ignored me and even somehow avoided all eye contact with me as we finished up with the last group people and made our way backstage.

After the concert we were loaded up onto the tour bus to hit east coast for more concerts and press. Neal wanted to meet again while we were doing a television show in Vermont to prepare us for give us our itinerary for the next few months. He took us out for lunch at this trendy Italian restaurant called Chow Bella. I sat with my back towards the window, watching the patrons make their way through the elongated dining area.

"Okay. I'm only going to say this one time. This set of interviews and press meetings are important. So don't be late!" Neal stressed. Directing his eyes towards me as well as Zack who recently got caught picking up a prostitute, he continued to explain how our image reflected on the record label. "No more dodging security or members of management. I want to know where you are every minute of the day. Remember, everything you do from now on will be viewed under a microscope. Keep the bad habits to minimum because I will not always be there to bail your asses out," he ended.

The fines were increasing and the tolerance level with my off stage antics decreased. I had to be extra cautious about the things that we did. Neal did not want any more bad press and neither did I.

We got to stay in Vermont for two days after hitting all of the talk shows and local radio stations. Chace, Jazz and I went to a local coffee shop to hang out and talk up our upcoming shows with security close by. Chace and Jazz found a booth in the corner of the coffee house as I made my way to other side of the bar to retrieve my beverage when I got the shock of my life.

I was dumbfounded by the dagger tattoo with a snake wrapped around it on the arm of a customer. I looked over at the stocky man with a short cropped salt and peppered hair as he began to speak.

"I remember you. It's been awhile," he said.

All I could do was stare with my mouth gaped as my worst nightmare stood in front of me. I quickly ran to the restroom to get away but it was no sanctuary as he followed me into the restroom.

"Elesin! Don't be rude. Didn't we teach you to respect your elders," he said as I walked backwards into the corner of the beige painted wall.

"Jake," I gasped. The closer he approached the more fear that surged through me. My body stiffened as he reached out to outline my face with his finger. "Don't..." I cried.

"Oh, don't be like that." he said as cupped my face in his right hand. "You grew up into a nice looking young man. Too bad – I'm only into younger boys." He released my face as the memories of what he and my uncle did to me returned. I closed my eyes as the images of the torture and rape flashed like super 8 mm film clicked through my mind.

I was overwhelmed with varying emotions that my legs began to give out from under me.

"Please leave," I whimpered as my body shook uncontrollably.

"Oh I will, I just wanted to say hi. It was really nice seeing you again," he said as he walked out with a smug look on his face.

The realization of what happened to me clutched my nerves. Seeing him brought back all the horrible memories from my childhood. I let out a piercing scream, dropping my body down onto the tiles. I closed my eyes tight, trying to erase the images of abuse from my mind. Holding myself, I dug my nails into my left arm until it bled. I scratched the pain away until I went numb.

Chace wondered into the restroom and immediately came to my aid.

"What's wrong?" Chace asked with visible concern. "What happened?"

"Don't come near me!" I screeched. "Don't touch me." I wailed as he continued to approach. I turned my body away from him as he reached out. It was all too much for me to handle and too much for me to process.

How was I to explain to Chace, my band mates that the site of my childhood rapist was here? Chace forcefully grabbed me from behind and healed me tight until I settled. Chace and I sat on the floor quietly with me trembling in his embrace. I rose to my feet and made my way to the sink to splash cool water onto my face. Looking at my reflection in the mirror, I saw Chace's eyes looking back at me with anguish and confusion as to what he just witnessed.

Later that night, I over indulged in mind altering substances in attempts at clearing my mind of all the images that I could not shake. Every time I closed my eyes – he was there. Jake, my uncles...were raping me all over again. I jumped into the shower to wash away my pain. Nothing I did could help erase the memories or the pain. I slip down the tiles of the shower and grabbed hold of my arm to calm myself. I didn't bother to bandage my arm after the shower and I just staggered to bed.

I was asleep when I got a call from Chace. I was mortified to discover that I had missed not one but three out of our five scheduled appearances.

"Where the hell have you been? We've been calling all day"

"I'm here, in my room."

"You're in your room?" Chace asked incredulously, obviously frustrated and upset. "You've been MIA for two days and you're in your room?"

"What? Two days?"

"What the fuck, man? You've really fucked up this time. We can't keep doing this shit, covering for you while you get high and party—"

"That's not what happened."

"Then what?"

"I don't know."

"What the fuck do you mean you don't know?" Chace's patience was growing thin. "Don't even give me that shit. C'mon dude, —I've had your back. As your friend, I deserve an explanation."

"I can't talk about this now. I just can't," I mumbled. "Just give me a moment to clear my head."

"I'm coming over. You don't sound too good, dude."

I tried to dissuade him from coming over, but it was a battle I could not win, so I propped the door open so he could just walk in when he arrived. Seriously hung over, I lay in the bed, hidden under the covers.

"Elesin?" Chace's voice echoed as he walked into my room, closing the door behind him. Unfortunately, he brought reinforcements.

"What the fuck? You're sleeping now?" Jazz shouted.

"I can't..."

"You can't what? Handle your drugs?" Jasper retorted. I heard his heavy footsteps approaching my bed. He yanked the covers off of my body. "Get up. Now! You have some explaining to do."

Not knowing what to say, my eyes red and swollen welled up with tears. Chace quickly came to my aid. "Dude, what's wrong? What happened?"

"I'll tell you what's wrong. He's a selfish prick who only thinks about himself and doesn't take responsibility for his actions," Zack scolded.

"No, that's not true. I swear."

"Then what?" Chace asked.

"I, ah—"

"Spit it out, ass hole!" Jazz pushed.

"I was fucking raped as a child..." I rose to my feet, standing face to face with Jazz. As I continued, "the man who nearly killed me, fucking cornered me in the restroom of that coffee house and I freaked, you asshole!" I screamed.

The looks on their faces were that of disbelief and shock. I curled back into bed, crying with a pillow covering my head, shielding my face, my shame, from their view. Chace curled up beside me in attempt to console me, but there was no comfort. The only thing running through my mind was that this would definitely not go over well with Neal. I was just too depressed to even care.

Whatever the situation, I had to compose myself enough to make the last two events on the schedule, the last being a concert. It took everything I had but I did it. I went onstage and let my emotion out in song. Soon after the performance, we were back at the hotel. Chace had stayed with me in my room, making sure that I was okay and on time for our last appearance. I just knew that once home, I would get an earful from the management team.

After the last obligation, I was on the next plane out. I was able to catch an earlier flight by not doing a meet and greet. I just did not feel like talking to anyone. I just wanted to be home, and hopefully Richard would be in a good mood.

I reluctantly told Richard what had happened to me. Naturally, he felt that it was my fault that I was raped. He was very disappointed with me, no sympathy or compassion. He even pushed me around a bit but nothing traumatizing. He had to go away for a few weeks and stressed that I was to get into no more trouble, no more men and no more parties. I was a grown ass man and I was grounded. Funny thing is it was fine with me.

I laid in bed trying to make sense of everything that happened to me over the years. Feeling more and more depressed as the day went on, I was overwhelmed by hatred. I hated my life, hated what had happened to me. I even hated what was to become of my future with the band. "How did it all get out of control?" I muttered.

Chapter 13
Making a Move

When Neal came over to my house and brought along my band mates, my wife, kids, a couple of men I had never seen before, my sister, hell, even Christian was here. I knew this was not going to be a good meeting. It felt like I had the weight of the world on my shoulders. They all made themselves comfortable as I stood in a corner, avoiding all eye contact.

Neal began. "I set up this meeting to let you know that we care for you too much to let you continue spiraling down this path. We have tried to reach out to you numerous times, to help you get out of this horrible situation. We no longer know what to do. I mean, look at yourself." Neal continued on with his rant. "You look like shit and your performances are for shit."

"What is this about?" I asked as I began to pace the floor, biting the bottom of my lip. "Is this some sort of intervention?"

"Yes. This is an intervention," Neal answered.

One of the men, Darryl Anderson, began to explain how he was a counselor at a treatment facility in New Mexico called the Life Healing Center. His assistant Chuck, I gathered, was there to make sure that I did not run. After they finished explaining treatments they provided and how it could help me, my mind just shut down.

Neal began to speak again. "You have been a part of this family for years and we are no longer going to stand by and watch you kill yourself with…whatever the hell you're on."

"Drugs are not the problem."

"Then what is? It's definitely something that is keeping you on this dangerous path, keeping you from seeing clearly and keeping you in this fucked up relationship with Richard." Neal continued to express his concern for my mental and physical health as the others looked on.

I shook my head, trying to figure out a way out of this madness. Neal continued. "This cannot go on anymore. We also cannot sit by and watch you in this abusive relationship, but that's for another day. Hopefully, when you accept the help that we're offering you, you will be able to put an end to all your bad habits."

It had been awhile since I'd been warned about my personal life and having it interfere with the business Neal had created for us. I was his business. I was his product.

"And if I don't?"

"If you don't, we will release you from your contract before we start working on the new album next year."

The ultimatum was reasonable. Either get into a program or be released from my contract. I also had to leave Richard and try to repair the burned bridges and focus on the success of the band.

"But I don't have a drug problem."

"Really?" Neal contested. "Then how do you explain your disappearances, your appearance at The Metro, the fact that you disappeared for two days with no memory of what happened? How about the fact that no one has seen you in over two weeks now? This is a recurrent theme."

I was being backed into a corner. I couldn't take it anymore and attempted to leave the room, but I was promptly blocked by Chuck. Turning my back to the men in the room, I was forced to listen to each member of N'Step speak about how much they cared and valued our friendship. All of them ended with, "We care deeply for you and we do not want to see you die."

I was leaning on the side of the stairs when my eight-year-old, Lynnea, approached me with a letter in her trembling hand. She had a somber look on her face as she read her feelings aloud and how she felt that I needed to get help.

"Daddy, I love you so much. I hate to see you hurt yourself..."Then my son Jerrod walked up to hold his sister's hand. I dropped to my knees, weakened by the barrage of emotional pleas. My children grabbed a hold of me to give me a hug. I held on for dear life, my life.

Kissing their cheeks, I whispered to them, "I'm so sorry I've failed you."

Chace walked over to me. He picked me up off the floor and led me to the sofa. I was defeated and overcome with emotion. Surveying the room, I realized I was surrounded by friends and family who cared for me. Yet, all I could think was, "How the hell can I get out of this?"

By the time MJ spoke, I had to leave the room. Close on my heels was Jazz, who hugged me from behind, whispering in my ear how much he loved me. It was all too much to bear. *Stupid, stupid boy.*

"Don't touch me! Don't any of you touch me!" I yelled.

"This is for your own good," Jazz comforted as I broke free from his grasp and made my way to the restroom. After splashing water on my face and composing myself, I hesitantly made my way back into the living room. I forced myself to listen as the other band mates expressed their feelings and encouraged me to get help.

"I don't know what to do," I cried.

"We are going to help you?"Jazz reassured.

"I can't do this now. Please don't make me do this now."

"If you don't do this, then you're out," Neal said matter-of-factually.

"Everyone get out!" I screamed. "Just go! I don't need any of you. No one here knows me or what I am going through. Drugs are not the issue here," I shouted, nearing hysterics.

Christian tried his best to console me, to calm me. He held me in his arms, whispering in my ear how much he loved me.

Zack was next to speak. He was infuriated by the events that had transpired in previous months as well as this last debacle. He ended with, "I am afraid that I can no longer be in your life if you do not get into a program."

Too defeated and too tired to even try to argue. What could I say? I knew that I was in a no-win situation. Jaelyn even promised to help me through it. The reoccurring theme that I was not alone, the endless amount of love being shared throughout the room was amazing. However, I have never felt so alone in my life. No one understood me, or maybe they did. I needed to be alone, to think. I headed back to the bathroom, with Christian and Jazz trailing behind. As I raised my shirt up to wipe away my tears, the healed bruises from one of Richard's rages were still visible.

"I will kick Richard's ass when I see him. He has no right to put his fucking hands on you like that," Christian said in a rage.

"You just don't understand," I cried.

"Fuck you, man. Don't you even tell us that you're staying in this fucked up relationship?" Jazz yelled after looking at my eyes. My mouth dropped open as Jazz continued. "You are a fucking idiot. Now I know why you're snorting that shit." Jazz stormed out of the room.

I dropped my head down not knowing how to explain the fear I felt in believing what Richard would do to me or my children if I ever left.

In frustration, Jazz came back and shouted back, "You're a dead man if you fucking stay here. You hear me? Dead! I cannot continue to witness your death."

I couldn't look him in the face. After a moment of dreadful silence, I could hear him leaving and slamming the front door. Christian kept holding on to me as we sat on the bathroom floor in silence.

"I can't do it," I whispered. "I'll do whatever you need me to do, but I cannot go to that treatment center."

The look on Christian's face said it all. Although he was disappointed with my decision, he stayed with me, making sure that I was all right. He was great that way, very nurturing and caring.

"Look at me," he said as he lifted my chin. "You are going to be okay. This program is not a prison sentence. We just want you to get some help. Por favor."

"I'll go crazy."

"Dude, you already are. We're all a bit crazy, but baby, you are scaring us. I don't want to wake up to see on the news that you have OD'd or worse."

"I'm afraid."

"Don't be."

"I can't do this. I'm not ready. I'm not strong enough." Christian shook his head, clearly disappointed as we made our way back to the living room. He informed everyone of my decision to forgo treatment.

The looks of disappointment were apparent.

"Think long and hard about what you're saying right now, Elesin. Think about your career. Think about your children for fuck sake," Neal advised.

"Do I need to make a decision now?"

"It would be best."

The ultimatum was reasonable. Either get into a program or be released from my contract. I also had to leave Richard and try to repair the burned bridges and focus on the success of the band. I inhaled deeply until I force myself to answer. "Okay, I'll do it."

Christian and Jaelyn helped me pack for my trip. I would be entering a four-week program for chemical dependency. As I kissed my family and friends good-bye, nothing more was said. On the drive to the airport, I looked out the window with the same feeling I had when I was six and being sent away from home.

The first night at the treatment center was a blur of information. The orientation was conducted by Chuck who gave me a full tour of the facility as well as my schedule for the week. "You will start out with our stabilization phase of the program, we need to monitor you while you detox. It may not hit you now but it will hit you. Breakfast is at 7:00 A.M. every day and group at 9:00 A.M." We continued walking down the hallway peering into each counseling area and treatment rooms. He talked about the activities I could do to past the time when not in session, then he stopped and looked at me sternly to say, "But you must attend group and individual counseling session."

My mind was whirling with ways of getting out of this situation. I looked around paying close attention to every exit. "Elesin? Are you listening?"

"What? Yes...Sorry." I answered quickly. My anxiety level rising to a noticeable degree as well walked down the hall. The beige colored walls closing in on me as we made it to my room.

"You will get through this. I promise," he said as he helped me get settled in my room, checking every bag, every item to ensure no illegal substances were present. As he left me alone, I sat at the end of my bed with my face in my hands, wondering how my life got to this point.

By day three, I had crashed – hard. I was hallucinating and seeing the images of my uncle and Jake entering my room. Each of the three days, I cried out in my sleep. I could feel those men touching me all over again, violating my body. On day five, I was so exhausted from lack of sleep that I was unsure of my surroundings.

It wasn't long after detoxing that I was well into my counseling sessions for sexual abuse. Week three in the four week program was one of the hardest and most revealing experiences I've ever had in my life. It was through my individual counseling sessions that it was realized I used drugs and sex as defense. The sexual abuse experienced during my developmental years made it hard for me to develop any kind of healthy relationship.

The four weeks came and went. Surprisingly, it wasn't as scary as I thought, but it was one of the hardest and most revealing experiences I've ever had. It was through my individual counseling sessions when it was realized that used drugs and sex as defense. The sexual abuse did during my developmental years made it hard for me to develop any kind of healthy relationship.

I worked on making myself a better person

and learn what love really means. I also got to work on more poetry and songs. During my final session, I decided with a heavy heart, that I would not continue with N'Step. While at the treatment center, I thought about the many stressors in my life. Aside from my domestic situation and past childhood trauma, being a part of a boy band and needing to assimilate within the groups dynamic was too much for me. I needed to be on my own.

Working on my own sound without having to worry if I was pissing someone off was something I needed to do. In the middle of November, I informed Diane of my plans to leave the group, to my surprise, Neal and the guys were actually very understanding. Neal had the papers drawn up to release me from my contract at the end of the year. There was a small fine involved, of course, but I would be free to focus on my next project, my solo project.

I had gotten a call from Sabrina Starr who wanted to see how I was doing and to also confirm that I was still performing in the showcases he and Bryan aka Hylan Parc were putting on. She was quite enthused that I had planned to perform and had my song ready.

The costume that I did not leave much to the imagination. It was a hot, silver number, very short, extra tight with a revealing midsection. The theme, Olivia Newton John.

Chace, who was also performing in the show as well, and decided to reserve spots for both of us in the center of the club for our friends and family. I informed Christian that he had to go. I wasn't going to take no for an answer.

"Anything to see you in drag, I'm all in." He laughed.

The night of the show, Chace and I met up in the dressing room. He looked like a gorgeous Greek statue, all painted in shimmery golden body glitter, sporting golden hot pants with spiked hair. He was looking "hawt."

I only had my face on while the others were performing. I was not going on until later in the evening, so I greeted my friends out front before show time. Christian was sitting at a reserved spot close to the bar. He got a kick out of my appearance. From the back, I looked like a regular guy in jeans, a hoodie and a baseball cap. From the front, all face—dramatic eyes, lips and glitter. *Gotta have sparkles, bitches.*

Nearing the time for my performance, I headed back stage to change into my barely there shimmery silver mini dress with matching bottoms. Abs exposed, check...platinum blonde Mohawk wig, check...I was ready.

The music cued, lights flashed and I was on. My song of choice was "Make a Move on Me." I slowed the tempo down for a sexier, rhythmical sound. Every word sounded orgasmic.

"I can tell you got plans for me, and your eyes are saying you made them carefully."

Slithering my way across the stage, I allowed my body to be free, swaying to the music. I owned the stage and made the audience feel each and every word, every gesture. After the first break

174

I jumped off the stage and headed toward Christian who was mesmerized and unable to take his eyes off me. He and everyone in the room began to realize who I was singing to. I stood directly in front of him, dropped to the floor, rose up sensually and worked my way up to his ear, breathing the next line:

"You made the prettiest speech I've heard, but a single touch surely is worth a   thousand words. To a heart that's open wide and from the start was on your side,"

Turning my back to him, I took his arms and wrapped them around me. I continued singing:

"Won't you spare me all the charms and take me in your arms, I can't wait, I can't wait. I'm the one you want, that's all I wanna be, so come on baby make a move on me."

He gasped and trembled with wonderment. As I sashayed my way back to the stage. I knew that I made my point and staked my claim. At the end of the song, the crowd roared, whistling and hooting in approval. I just hoped that it worked. I hoped that he was ready.

After the show, it was hard for Christian and me to keep our hands off of each other. "I think that I officially have a crush on Ferocia Couture," he said. I laughed and made my way through the crowds, taking pictures and signing autographs for the masses.

During the drive to the hotel, Christian and I made out until the driver got us to our destination. On our way up to the room, not much was said.

Clothes were being tossed from one side of the suite to the other. Collapsing onto the large sofa with him falling on top of me felt so right, so good. It was truly magical. Christian kept true to his Puerto Rican roots. Uninhibited. Passionate. Everything we had bottled up inside, was released with an earth-shattering, orgasmic explosion.

We laid in each other's arms, taking in each other's love, each other's soul. Then Christian asked, "Are you going to leave Richard?"

"I...I don't know. I'm not sure I can."

Without hesitation, he said, "Yes, you can. Tell me why it's so hard to leave him?" I could not possibly explain the relationship Richard and I shared.

"He helped me when no one else would. When I ran away from home, he was there for me. I just owe him a lot."

"Come on, you've got to do better than that. I was under the impression that we were going to build some sort of relationship?"

"I don't know if I can explain it, but I do want a relationship with you. I want nothing more than to have a life with you."

"Well, start explaining. We've just had a beautiful moment and leaving Richard is not an option? I deserve to know why."

Taking a deep breath and looking deep into Christian's eyes, I;m sorry. I just can't right now but I promise you, one day I will."

Christian's eyes rolled as he grumbled some choice words in spanish. Even though my silence frustrated him, he leaned in and offered to help me in any way that he could to help purge myself from Richard. We both knew that was not an easy task, but I had to try if I wanted a relationship with Christian. I reassured him that I was ready to make that change but I needed time.

"Christian, I have always loved you from the first moment that I saw you on the beach that day. Just give me time to get out," I said with pleading eyes.

I was surrounded by the comforting cream and white sheets on the bed and the strong brown arms of the man that I loved. I could not help but smile with I looked at him but I also knew that starting a relationship with Christian at this time would not be fair to him.

The roaming shadows of light rolling across the ceiling keeping my mind at peace until he responded.

"I've loved you since Mexico as well. I was just too afraid to admit it. That's why I wrote those songs for you." Christian held me in his arms.

"And I did love those songs mi amor. I knew you had written them for me," Christian squeezed me snuggly within his arms. He nestled his nose against the back of my neck causing goose bumps to form along my skin.

I tried drifting off to sleep but all I could think of was how I was going to leave Richard. I needed to figure out a way to break the news to him without him doing me harm. Christian's body pressed against me and I held his hand against my chest and fell asleep.

Waking up with Christian next to me was a

welcomed treat. Even in his sleep, he was sexy as hell. I got myself up to take a much needed shower. Adjusting the water temperature, I started singing, feeling for the first time that I was doing something right with my life. I knew right away what I had to do, and how.

Christian surprised me by entering the shower with me. "Buenos dias, mi amor," he said.

"Morning," I giggled as he squeezed me softly from behind, almost taking my breath away. He tickled my neck with his nose. "Quit it," I squealed.

"Make me," he challenged as he nestled me more.

It was on. I leaned back, rubbing myself into his bare chest. We enjoyed and explored every crease and every curve of our bodies, lathering each other with soap. My head whirled with emotions I hadn't felt in a long time, feelings I had not felt since I was thirteen, when I first thought I was in love.

My body pressed against the frosted glass of the shower, I was weakened as his lips and tongue lick explored every inch of my body. The next thing I knew he was giving me a rimming that made my eyes roll to the back of my head, stopping just before I was about to come on the glass.

The pulsing water beat upon our bodies as he stuck his cock up my ass, thrusting rhythmically as I moaned with pleasure. I matched his staccato rhythm and grabbed his ass to pull him deeper inside me. He in turn pumped faster and deeper until an explosion of orgasmic surges coursed throughout our bodies. Christian's body collapsed onto mine as we both panted and our bodies rippled with aftershocks.

I decided to break up with Richard over the phone while he was away on business. I figured that it would be safer and hopefully easier if he wasn't near. I could only imagine what he would do if I broke things off in person. It took me three days before I could build up enough courage to make that call. But I had to do it. I was just tired of being a punching bag and a victim. I needed to think about my life, the lives of my children, even the one I was having with Tiffy.

As expected, Richard was not too happy.

"You're doing this now?" he barked.

"Yes, it's the only way. I just can't deal with this anymore."

"Right. Who is he? I know who, you're leaving me for that trick Chace?"

"No, it's not Chace and I just want out of this relationship. Please don't make this harder than it has to be."

"After everything that I've done for you? If I didn't come for you when I did, you wouldn't be here. You'd still be in your uncle's basement, tied up, raped or worse... dead."

"I know," I sobbed. "And I'm grateful for that. I—"

"Do this and I will make you pay!"

"Haven't I already paid with broken bones, blood and tears? What more do you want from me? I've got nothing left to give. I don't want to be with you anymore. I can't love you anymore." My voice cracked. "Please just let me go."

He laughed heartily. "Sorry, but I just can't do that. I won't do it."

It was hard for me not to shed tears, but he was a piece of my heart that I had to rip out. We argued for another ten minutes before I urged him not to come home. I also informed him that I had changed the locks on the doors. When the call ended, I realized that aside from going into that treatment facility, this was the hardest thing I'd ever done. But it was the best thing that I ever did.

Chapter 14
The New Year

I awoke with a feeling of weightlessness for the first time in my life and I was excited to start my life over. The year was winding down and I only had a couple more gigs with N'Step to fulfill my obligation. It would be sad ending the N'Step chapter of my life, but change would be good.

Out of the blue, I received a call from my father wanting to do lunch with me. He had been in New York on business and said he needed to discuss some things with me. We met at Nobu, a Japanese restaurant that is popular for those who enjoy fine cuisine and a cozy environment. The trendy eatery is absolutely beautiful with remnants of a Japanese countryside, birch trees, wood floors and a wall made of river stones. I had arrived early and had been studying the menu when he came.

He wore a tailored charcoal gray Armani suit, with a blush colored tie. Combed back, his blonde hair touched the top of his collar. I had forgotten how breathtakingly handsome he was, and everyone around us seemed to notice as well. I rose to greet him as he embraced me warmly in his arms.

"How have you been, son?"

"I'm doing well, for the most part." I forced a smile.

His right eyebrow raised with suspicion as the waiter took our orders.

"Sorry it's been awhile since I've contacted you. I just never knew how to approach you or when to, for that matter."

Bullshit. My father was so full of shit, but I still loved him just the same. I wished that we had some semblance of a normal father-son relationship, but that was not the case.

"Why now? What was so important that you needed to contact me now?"

He took a moment before responding. While he sipped his Spiced Pear Martini, I fidgeted around with the napkin that was in my lap. Then he finally spoke.

"Elesin, a lot of things have happened since you left home. I don't know if you know this, but your Uncle Sebastian's had not been seen since you left. Seemingly he went on a business trip and never—"

Holding up my hand to stop him from going further, I interrupted. "You're not saying that I had anything to do with his disappearance, are you? It's been over seven years. Why are you telling me this now?"

Alexander laughed, catching me off guard. "No, I'm not saying that you did. That somehow fell on Marta who, let's face it, was a mental basket case. I'm telling you this because you needed to know. You also need to know that I, well, I love you and I want to try to build a relationship with you."

"I'm sorry. Wait. What do you mean it *fell on*

her?" I was overwhelmed but the vast amount of information I was receiving – seven years worth.

I listened intently as my father broke down the sequence of events of how after I ran away to Mexico, Sebastian disappeared and was no longer seen again. A month after his disappearance, Marta was seen acting stranger than usual and began ransacking the house and tossing things out on the lawn.

Someone called the police to investigate the sudden disappearance of Sebastian and followed an incoherent Marta down into the basement when they discovered his body.

"Marta swore up and down that she had nothing to do with his death and could prove it, but no one listened. She was out of her mind. She did some time in Kingston up in Ontario." I was shocked by his revelation, speechless actually. The waiter brought our meals and placed them before us. I nearly choked off the noodles from my Seafood Udon when my dad said, "She didn't kill your uncle."

"How do you know?" I managed to ask.

"Remember that night I visited you with those papers for your uncle to sign?"

"Yes."

"I had known something was wrong. I just could not put my finger on what it was. It was when Richard had come to me and told me what my brother was doing to you..." He shook his head as if he were trying to erase the memory from his mind. "I wasn't there for you like I should have been and I am truly sorry for that." A single tear fell from the corner of my father's eye. Witnessing that vulnerability, I cried. No words could express the feelings that I felt at that moment.

Breaking the silence I finally asked, "Did you kill him?"

"I did what I thought was right at that time. When I saw the pictures and the movies, I was sickened. I had to burn them all. I didn't want anyone to know what that man had done to you, what I allowed. I saw how Richard and you looked at each other. I knew that helping you get away and live the life that you were entitled to was the best thing I as a father I could do for you." Both of our faces were soaked with tears. "I do love you and I will use all of my resources to keep you protected, even if I can't do it myself."

This was something that I had longed for and waited for all my life, the moment when my father would come back into my life and acknowledge his son with acceptance and love. He may not have been present in my childhood, but he had done more for me behind the scenes than I could have ever imagined and nothing could take that away from me.

Richard paid me a surprise visit in New York while the boys and I were doing a Christmas show at Madison Square Garden, my last show with the group. It was an emotional performance for not only the fans but for us as well.

After the show, the guys and I went backstage and sat down to recuperate after our high energy performance. People were still frantically moving around tearing down the set and packing up the gear.

I had gotten out of my stage clothes and put on something more comfortable, jeans and a Christian Ayala limited edition concert tee shirt. We were getting ready to meet up with the fans for my farewell autograph and interview session with the press.

Chace and I were goofing around as we walked down the hallway that lead to the main backstage lobby area to meet up with the other band-mates when I was stunned by the sight in front of me.   Richard, stood there with a bouquet of flowers in his hand. He was there attempting to apologize to me and my band mates for all the wrong he had done. Naturally, the guys were not very accepting nor welcoming to Richard and his empty promises to never hurt me again.

I wasn't thrilled to see him either and the mood changed quickly as I refused the flowers. The air was so thick with tension that Zack asked if he should have security on standby.

Richard approached me for a hug and I pushed him away.

"What? I can't even get a hug?" he asked.

"It's not that, but you shouldn't be here. How did you even get backstage?"

"That's not important. The important thing is that we have to try to repair our relationship before it's too late. We've been together for too long for something like your infidelity to break us up."

I stood stunned with my jaw dropped. I could not believe the gall.

"Are you fucking kidding me? Infidelity broke us up! Fuck you, Richard!" I walked off toward the commissary area with Richard following close behind. I wanted to be away from the crowd of fans that was starting to grow and media personnel who would certainly get an earful and sensational sound bites.

"I guess you have a different opinion."

"Uh...yeah! You beat the shit out of me. Remember? That's why we are no longer together. You did this, not me or my infidelity." I walked off to a more private area near the restroom and maintenance hallway, waving off my band mates who were on high guard.

"So I'm the blame?"

"Yes!" I gasped. "I can't fucking do this right now. I have to get ready to meet the fans and do an interview. Just stay away from me." Richard began to pace the floor with his fists balled. *Shit, he's gonna kill me,* I thought to myself. I threw my hands up and braced myself for what was to come. Just then Jazz rushed over, ready to take Richard down.

"Just give me five minutes—" Richard begged.

I glared at him. "I don't have five minutes to give. Please, just go away. Leave me alone."

"Baby, I'm so sorry," he said as he swiped away at tears. "You have to know that I would never harm you again. I promise."

I turned to Jazz who was a muscular six-foot-tall Italian who looked as if he would have no problems challenging Richard as he puffed out his chest.

"It's okay, Jazz. I'll be fine."

"Are you sure?"

"Yes, just let me handle this myself." The last thing I wanted was to create an even bigger scene.

As Jazz backed away, he looked at Richard shaking his head. Then he turned back to issue Richard a warning, "You touch him or harm him in any way and I swear to God I'll beat the living shit outta you." Both he and Zack stepped outside to give us some privacy.

Zack, who maintained his hip-hop style with a faded hair cut and dressed head-to-toe in FUBU, kept his eyes on Richard the whole time. I took the flowers from Richards hand as he began pleading his case. He about to explain why we should be together when Chace walked up beside me and placed his hand at the small of my back and whispered into my ear, "Let's go."

This infuriated Richard who, in a rage, stepped up to me. "How dare you flaunt your new toy in my face."

"What the fuck are you talking about?"

Richard pushed Chace down onto the floor with such force that hit his head onto the wall. Chace ran out off to go get Jazz for assistance.

"What the hell!" I yelled.

"You know exactly what I'm talking about," he growled, as he rushed me like a linebacker and pushed me hard against the wall.

"Don't do this," I yelled. "You promised—"

"I promised? You promised me that you

would be faithful. You promised me that you'd never flaunt your lovers in my face."

Zack and Jasper quickly ran over us to intervene to keep the peace.

"I think you need to leave," Zack suggested as he stepped between us. Zack wasn't that tall but he was scrappy and was stronger than he appeared.

"Yes, just go away, please," I begged, embarrassed beyond belief. I fought the tears that were welling up in my eyes.

"I don't think so." Like a ninja, Richard grabbed me by the arm and drug me into the restroom and locked the door. It happened so fast. My band mates began pounding on the door. I was able to fight off some of Richards blows, but I was never a match. It was never a fair fight. Richard kept punching me with heavyweight blows and spouted every derogatory he could think of.

"You selfish bastard!" He yelled.

I hollered for dear life, kicking and biting him in attempt to free myself from his grasp. By the time Jazz burst through the door, Richard had a death grip on my neck. I gasped to catch my breath but it felt like he was choking the life out of me.

"Get your fucking hands off of him!" Jazz commanded as he charged Richard who had me on the floor. It took three band mates and security to pull him off of me. Chace and MJ helped pull me away as Richard continued fighting his way free.

I stumbled out the room with MJ's assistance as we tried to find a place out of the media's view.

Everything was getting hazy. I was confused, my lip was bleeding and I was visibly shaken. Parents were clearly in shock as they attempted to shield their children eyes from this madness.

Jazz yelled, "MJ get him out of here!"

I guess three men could not keep this enraged man down. As Jazz, Zack and Chace tried to restrain Richard, somehow he broke free. Everyone watched the spectacle that was taking place. Several people were on cell phones calling the police while others were trying to take pictures. Richard bypassed security and pushed MJ out of the way, and returned me back into a headlock. My feet were barely touching the ground as Richard tightened his choke hold.

"Let him go, fucker!" MJ ordered.

"Call the cops! Someone call the fucking cops."

"Get…off!" I struggled to say.

Security and MJ struggling to break his arm free from my neck as I began to struggle less. I heard sirens coming closer as the fire exit doors crept open. The screams of the onlookers grew louder. Then finally I was freed as the cops unleashed 1500 volts of electricity into Richard's body.

MJ and Zack held me up as I fought for air. "Never again!" I gasped. "Never, again!"

As the police officers cuffed Richard and began to take him away, he grunted, "This is not over."

"It is so fucking over! I'm so fucking done!" I yelled as my voiced cracked. I was so upset and embarrassed by what had transpired, I cried, "I can't go through this shit anymore. You stay the fuck away from me."

"You'll be sorry. I will make you pay!"

"Leave him alone. Don't you dare try to threaten him," Chace shouted back as the officers drug Richard away.

Richard hollered, "I've fucking killed for you. You cannot fucking leave me until I say."

I was devastated, mortified. It was one thing to have everything happened behind closed doors, but in front of fans, journalists and my band mates? And what the fuck? He's killed for me.

The EMT's checked me out to make sure that I wasn't seriously hurt. Later, police took our statements and I filed assault charges on Richard. My mind was preoccupied with what Richard had said, though. *He's fucking killed for me. Who did he kill for me? Sebastian? Is that what my father meant?*

My band mates came up to me to ensure that I was okay, offering their friendship and support to me if needed. I was very lucky. I never saw it before, but they were my family and always would be. I never realized just how important they were in my life.

"Thank you guys so much for everything," I said as all four men looked on. "I know that this was our last show together and I never said it before but I appreciate everything that you guys have done for me. I love each and every one of you." I couldn't suppress the tears from running down my face.

"Don't cry. It's all good. We love you, too,"

Jazz said.

"Yeah, we're your brothers and always will be," Zack said as he pulled me into his arms for a much needed hug. The others followed suit.

"I have treated you guys like shit. I wish that I didn't close myself off from you guys. I wish I had gotten to know you better."

"Don't worry. We have plenty of time to get to know each other and bond," Zack reassured. I continued thanking them for the support and for helping me through the Richard situation.

By 10:30, my journey as a member of N'Step was over. I was starting the New Year—a new year free from N'Step...free from Richard.

Happy fucking New Year to me.

Chapter 15
OMG!

"Guess who just got kicked out of the closet? Elesin Vollan, the twenty-four-year-old heartthrob had a very public, very violent altercation with his boyfriend 36 year old Richard Shuffer after a holiday concert this weekend.

Although Vollan nor his reps have confirmed the pairs relationship, it is apparent from the amateur videos shot from fans that their relationship has ended. Whether personal or professional, the argument quickly turned violent and had to be broken up by police and security. We will keep you posted on more news as we get it on the Insider."

It had been two weeks since my very public assault at the hands of my ex-lover.
Christian, who had relocated to Miami, suggested that I stay with him until things in the press died down. Naturally, when he asked, it didn't take much for me to take him up on his offer, temporarily. He also advised me to get a restraining order on Richard. I explained that that while it sounded good on paper, but nothing would stop Richard from coming after me again.

Christian not only had a huge album out, but he had planned a huge New Year's eve party in

Miami before taking off again on a promoting tour in L.A. He tried to spend as much time with me as he could, but I have to admit, I wasn't much fun. I just could not get out of my depressed mood. Seeing my attack being replayed on every news station and all over the Internet did not help.

After a couple weeks, things were better. Christian and I got to hang out on a full time basis and our relationship was developing into a into something more serious.

As I stood out on his deck, enjoying Miami's beauty, Christian hugged me and said, "You should really consider moving down here."

"Yeah right."

"No, seriously. Think about it. You can also stay here...with me... until you figure out what you want to do," he offered. I couldn't help smiling. A fresh new start was definitely what I needed. Just looking at Christian made me smile. He leaned into me and said, "You know how much I love you?"

I smiled, taking in his beautiful eyes, lips, and his entire face. I'd make sure that he knew how much I loved him...over and over again. I was excited not only for the future but the future I was starting with Christian.

Christian and I were off to L.A. I was staying in a hotel trying to plot my next move while he met with a couple of producers regarding his new album. After the meeting, he was going to be in D.C. for his charity organization for a week. While he was away, I locked myself away in my room attempting to keep away from outside influences. I just needed to be alone to think. I stayed away from the phone and television for six days before tuning back into the world. I just knew that my voicemail box was full.

As soon as I turn my cell back on, it rang. It was Mitchel. He had heard about my little incident with Richard and wanted to know if I were okay. He also added, "I am so glad to hear that you are free from that fucking blood sucking bastard." He had a way with words.

"Better late than never."

"No shit, he was really no good for you.

"I know." Mitchel wanted to meet with me and hang out for brunch. I was all in. We met at a Starbucks to discuss everything that was going on in our lives. I sat attentively listening to Mitchel's stories. Remembering all the fun we had and thinking about what could have been. I had missed him so much and wanted to maintain our friendship. While I playing catch up with Mitchel, Christian was getting ready for his return back to L.A. to meet with me. He also needed to go back into the studio to rework some of the songs he had recorded.

Mitchel and I sat and chatted about our plans for the future. Mitchel confessed that he was thinking about switching gears and getting out of theater but was unsure what he wanted to do. I informed him that I'd be moving in with Christian in Miami.

"You could definitely use a fresh new start. Lawd knows you deserve it," Mitchel laughed.

"What are your plans for this month?" I asked.

"Well, I'm going away myself. Germany. I

will be touring with another production company to do the musical Hair," he smiled.

"Nice." Mitchel was obviously glad that I had left Richard and did not hold any hard feelings towards me. Surprising since I was the cause of him getting assaulted. I was relieved that we could maintain and continue our friendship. We hung out for about two hours before parting ways.

Once in my car, Christian, who was in flight, called to check up on me. "What are doing?"

"Well, I just meet with Mitchel for brunch and now I am going to the house to get some things of mine, legal documents that I needed."

"I don't think that you should be going to the house along. What if he's there?" Christian was concerned. He did not think it was wise for me to go back to the house at all.

"I'll be fine." I tried reassuring him as well as myself the best that I could, that nothing bad was going to happen. "Besides, he should be at work and I did change the locks. The house should be empty."

"How about this? I will meet you at the house and we can go in together," he offered. "Please, just wait for me. I do not want you to go to that fucking house alone."

"Christian, I'll be okay. Just get back soon and we can get on with our lives."

"Fine, but if you get into any trouble at all call me. I will be in L.A. in thirty minutes. When we ended our call, I had second thoughts about going into the house. Maybe I should stop being so impatient and wait on Christian. I just wanted to get in, get out and on with my life. I should be fine.

Once at the house. I paused at the door. I listened for any signs of life, of movement, but there was none. I ran upstairs, packed up a few personal items and retrieved my documents out of the safe. With a stuffed duffel bag over my shoulder, I headed down the stairs but was startled at the sight of Richard, in his underwear.

"Leaving so soon?" He asked as he blocked the door. I didn't know how to respond, my anxiety levels rose as time seemed to slow down.

"Hey baby. I was just grabbing some things--" I dropped the bag at the bottom of the stairs, and approaching him with open arms. Richard, stood still with a twisted smile on his face.

"Don't!" He snapped holding up his hand. Dropping my arms. Frozen with anticipation of what was to come. He continued, "After all that I had done for you. And you have the audacity to leave me without saying goodbye."

"No! That's not it. It's just--"

Cutting me off, "You have never thought about anyone but yourself. You never cared about me."

"No, I was going to call you. I just needed time to think. That's all." I tried backing away. The gleam in his eyes was gone and his expression changed. It transformed into something I did not recognize. Sensing the danger, I backed away from him towards the kitchen. Attempting to exit out the back door, but it was locked.

"Humph! Would you look at that? It's locked." Richard said from behind holding the key to the lock in his hand. "Remember what I told you? What I told you I would do if you left me?" Then I heard a sound, so chilling, so frightening. I was paralyzed with fear.

It was the sound of a knife being removed from the butchers block. Just as I was beginning to turn around, the blade came down on my right shoulder. The force and impact so great, I slammed into the door I was trying to escape through.

"No!" The wind being knocked out of me with each vicious attack. Falling to my knees.

"The only way you will leave me...this house, is in a fucking body bag." He said calmly as the knife plunged into my flesh, hitting in several areas of my back, then chest. I reached out my hand to block the blows. He lowered his face close to mine and said, "I loved you. I killed for you and I didn't get some much as a thank you for saving your life." The blade driving slowing into my stomach.

As he removed the knife, he stood up. I mustered every ounce of deteriorating strength in my body and was able to kick his knee and force him down to the ground. I scrambled up as best as I could., trying to make my way to the front door. I was losing blood fast as I stumbled in a horrified panic, trying to get away. I failed miserable as he tackled me to the floor. Screaming for someone to help. Screaming for him to stop. I managed to elbow him in the groin and quickly made my way to door. With my wet, bloodied hands, it was hard to open the door. Richard pounced on me with little effort and straddled my body.

"Please, just stop." I pleaded.

"You stop. Just stop fighting. It will be over soon."

"I'm sorry! I'm sorry I betrayed you." Lying flat on my back. Richard, kissed my lips for the last time. Rising to his knees. The knife held high and coming down so fast, so hard to the chest. My body went numb and I blacked out.

I was awakened by the ringing of a phone…my phone. Unsure of how long I was lying on the floor. The only thing I knew was that I was in tremendous pain, I was bloody and I was weak. I crawled my way to the door and somehow managed to get it open. I heard screams and shouting from what seemed like every direction.

I took several steps towards the gate and fell to the ground. I heard a commotion but my vision was blurred and my breathing labored. My vision was getting fuzzy and then there was nothing.

Dispatcher: 911 emergency…

Paparazzi: I am at Elesin Vollan's house at 11190 Hollwood Hills, …He has been attacked in his home. It looks like his been stabbed several times.

Dispatcher: Is he breathing?

Paparazzi: Yes. There is so much blood. Get someone out here quick.

Calls flooded the emergency hotline with calls for help. My brutalized body was surrounded by a pool of blood as hordes of paparazzi gathered. Some rendering aid and others taking pictures and video as the ambulance, fire and rescue, and police secured and controlled the scene.

Chapter 16
Reunion

Breaking news. Twenty-four-year-old pop star Elesin Vollan has been brutally attacked in his Hollywood Hills home. It is unclear at this time if this was a home invasion or a domestic assault. Elesin had been living here with what appears to be his long time domestic partner
Richard Shuffer who was not present once rescue crews arrived.

Elesin has been taken to Valley Trauma Center and was listed in critical condition when he arrived. We will keep you posted with more information as it becomes available...Keep it here on Inside News for late-breaking celebrity news.

Christian ran frantically through the airport fighting through the crowd trying to find a car. He had just deplaned and saw that news ticker on CNN, which was being broadcasted on every television in the airport.

Finally flagging down a cab, he hopped inside and said, "Valley Trauma Center. Make it fast."

The crowds grew outside the hospital, awaiting news of my condition. When Christian approached the reception area looking for any news, he was met by Chace and my sister Dehlia.

"How is he? Have you heard anything?" Christian asked with shear fear and panic.

Dehlia answered, "It seems that he was stabbed several times. They are still working on him but we won't know anything until he's out of surgery."

"Oh my God, it's all my fault...I should have made him wait for me," Christian huffed. In frustration.

"It's not your fault," Chance consoled. "No one could have predicted this."

"I know but I could have gone with him."

Everyone trying to figure out what happened. Hours had passed when Dr. Nelson came out into the waiting room.

"Does Elesin's have any family here?"

"Yes, I'm his sister," Dehlia answered. The looks of shock and low mumblings filled the room as Dr. Nelson led Dehlia though the double doors to fill her in on what was going on.

"What the fuck?"

"Did you know that was his sister?"

"Hell, I've known Elesin for years and I had no clue," Christian confessed as he paced the room. "Fuck! I've known her for years. She never--he never," he ended. Confused by the revelation.

Just then Dehlia returned to the waiting room to inform everyone that I was recovering from fifteen stab wounds.

"Fortunately, his vital organs were not hit." She went on to say that he lost a lot of blood and was unsure when he would awaken.

"Can I see him?" Christian asked.

"Only family--" she stopped. "Guess you can be our brother. They will let us back once he is in recovery.

Chace was the first to ask Dehlia why neither of us shared with them that we were siblings.

"I mean are you two really related or was that just a lie you told the doctors to see Elesin?"

She smiled, "We are really brother and sister; twins actually."

"Twins!" Both Christian and Chace repeated. Christian sat down on the uncomfortable blue chair.

"It's just not something that we advertise. I mean basically, it's no one's business," she ended.

"This is too much but I don't understand how you can be twins? Aren't you younger?" Christian asked.

Dehlia shrugged and diverted her attention towards the people passing by the lobby area. Christian rolled his eyes and laughed until he was in tears, upset with everything that transpired. It was too much for anyone to handle as Chace and Dehlia comforted him. More and more people arrived to the lobby awaiting news of my condition. Diane was chatting with her ex-assistant Dehlia when the rest of my ex-band mates arrived.

I woke up to the smell of fresh flowers and familiar cologne. Slowing opening my eyes I winced in pain and tried to focus. I looked around the sterile hospital room and saw Christian in the corner sleeping on the sleeper. My body was stiff and sore. My leg bandaged from the knife wound to the hamstring. Guess I got that one from my failed attempts to get away. My right shoulder was bandaged just as tightly as my leg. Guess I got that one from my failed attempts to get away. The door creaked as it open and in stepped my sister. Suddenly I heard someone entering the room. I looked over.

"Dehlia." My voice dry and hoarse.

"How are you feeling Ales?"

"Feels like I've been stabbed multiple times."

"Humph." She shook her head as she approached with flowers in hand. "That's not funny."

"I know. I'm sorry."

"You know. He hasn't left your side since you've been here," she smiled, looking over at Christian. "He must really love you."

"He does. More than you'll ever know." I snapped as she continued to arrange the flowers in the room. "Did they get Richard?"

"No. They can't find him." My heart sank. Suddenly I was filled with fear and anxiety of what could happen once Richard realized I wasn't dead. Would he come back to finish the job?

Christian shifted his weight, then opened his eyes.

"Hey baby. You're awake," I smiled as Christian began to approach my bed.

"Hey, how are you feeling?" he asked as he kissing my forehead.

"I'll leave you two alone." Dehlia placed some flowers in an unoccupied spot on the table.

"I'll tell everyone you're awake." When she left, Christian planted the biggest and most passionate kiss on me. She was careful not to press against me too hard.

"I was so afraid that I was going to lose you. I'll take good care of you from now on." He promised.

"Okay, I'll let you. And I promise to be good to you my love."

Christian and I continued talking about who was in the waiting room waiting see me when an unexpected visitor entered the room.

My eyes widened in shock.

"Mother?"

"Ales. I see you are doing well."

"Yes, as well as can be expected." As she looked at Christian I quickly introduced her to him. She nodded in his direction. Wow. My mother had come to visit. I was so shocked by the arrival that I could barely speak. *Why was she here? Did she really care?* Her questions were more like an interrogation than questions of concern.

"Ales, there are some discrepancies with your paperwork and your identification." Mother began talking to me as if we were strangers rather than mother/son. "I keep telling the doctors and the administrators that you are not twenty five years old," she continued.

Christian's eyebrows rose as he listened on. I just laid there mortified, wondering what else she's disclosed.

"So, how old are you really?" Christian asked.

"He's only twenty one." Nyla answered before I could get a word out.

"What!" Christian gasp in shock. Trying to compute the revelation.

I just rolled my eyes at my mother and promptly turned my attention to Christian.

"I'm so sorry. I had to lie about my age to get here." Raising his hand to stop me from talking.

"What else did you lie about?"

"Nothing that would affect us I swear." I looked over at Christian who was now smoothing out the sheet draped over me.

"So you are still spreading your lies to everyone who will listen. Silly boy."

"Mother! Just stop."

"Did he tell you why he was kicked out of the house at twelve?" Nyla asked with a devilish grin.

"Please. Why are you doing this? Why are you even here?" I asked.

"Well, I thought that if you were in a bad way that I'd see you once before--"

"I died?"

"Yes, but that's not the only reason"

How typical. Nyla never did love me. I don't know why I expected that fact to change over time. She never showed much affection toward me as a child, why would this be any different?

"So, what's the other reason," I asked.

"Ales," she sang.

"Ugh! I hate it when you call me that," I snapped.

"Okay, Elesin. Contrary to what you

204

believe, I do love you. I just didn't know how to handle you or your—homosexual tendencies."

She looked over at Christian who was quietly absorbing everything being said.

She continued, "I still don't understand it nor do I care too but I just thought that you should know that."

She leaned over to place a kiss upon my cheek and swiped the stray hair from my brow.

"My little green-eyed boy." When she said that, I closed my eyes and remembered how her voice comforted me when I was young. If only I could feel the same way with her, feel the connection—but I couldn't, she was a stranger to me.

"Well mother. It was nice seeing you but I'm pretty tired now." I was nowhere near tired but I didn't not know how to get her out of my room. She shot a quick look across to Christian and began slowly walking towards the door.

She turned and said, "By the way Marta had found me. She wants to see Lynnea," Nyla added as she looked at Christian for a reaction.

"Who cares!" I snapped. "I will never allow her anywhere near Lynnea."

"She is her mother. She has every right. Did you tell Christian here that you snatched Lynnea away from her mother without warning?" She continued.

"Mother don't!"

"Don't what?" she pushed. "Don't tell everyone that you ran off with a mothers child."

"Don't do this now. I can't do this now."

Christian was getting an earful. His eyes filled with questions.

"What the fuck is going on here?" Christian asked.

"What's going on is that Elesin is a liar and kidnapper." Nyla ranted.

"Mother! Shut it!"

"You shut it. You stop lying. It will end here."

"Just leave. I cannot handle this right now," I grumbled. I could not believe my mother had the audacity to show up with this shit. "Just go away and stay away."

"Oh but you can handle running off with a man who helped you steal money from your father and steal a child from her mother?" She just would not let up. I was just too tired to argue any more.

"Mother!" I interrupted as I became more annoyed and frustrated with the situation. "Why are you really here? To ruin my life?" She just smiled as she shifted around the floral gifts and stuffed bears.

"Hey let's not do this now. Your son has been through a lot? He needs his rest." Christian interjected. Nyla smirked, she clearly did not like that he interrupted.

"I'll guess I'll leave you two alone. Apparently you have a lot to discuss with Christian as well as the police," she added.

"Mother, just go now!"

"Ales, the lies end here." She ended as she marched out the room.

"Damn it!"

Christian walked over to the door. Locking us in the room for privacy.

"Explain yourself?" Christian asked with obvious concern. "Why did you have everyone thinking that you were older than you were? Why would you lie about that?"

"Please, don't be upset, but I had to do it in order to leave home and live a somewhat normal life," I answered.

"Why did you have to lie about your age?" I had to do damage control. The last thing that I wanted to do was ruining my relationship with Christian. As I explain, the look in Christian's eyes changed back to the loving, concerned look that I was familiar with. I told him everything sparing no detail. He began to truly understand the relationship I had with Richard. Began to understand why it was so hard for me to leave.

Answering questions from the cops took a lot out of me. They wanted to know everything from the nature of me and Richard's relationship to how the assault was initiated. Once the details of my attack were known, the press was all over it. Turning on the television there was no surprise that I was the subject of every news station.

"Today on Inside News, our top story involves ex-N'Step member, Elesin Vollan. Vollan's life before N'Step has always been somewhat of a mystery but details are finally beginning to surface. The former lead singer of N'Step has never publicly come out but after he was viciously attacked in his home by Richard Shuffer, his longtime boyfriend.

According to Vollan's estranged mother,
Nyla Benet, her son ran away from home with
Shuffer when he was fourteen-years-old. The then
twenty-eight-year-old financial consultant, aided in
creating a life with his under-aged lover.

 More and more information is coming out
about the pop star twenty-one-year-old pop star...

 We will keep you updated with the latest
news about the life of the young star as it becomes
available. Keep it here on your Inside News for
your celebrity news. Next..."

"Great!" I grumbled as Christian and I
watched aghast at the information being sent out
across the world. I had to do some damage control
with not only with the press but my friends as well.
I had to also keep the masses from discovering what
had happened to me as a child. I just was not ready
for that.

 Over the next few days, I was able to see
more visitors. Even my absentee father paid me a
visit. Christian was awestruck as he saw this
gorgeous platinum blonde haired man enter the
room.

 "I can see where you got your looks from,"
Christian blushed. My father smiled and extended
his hand to Christian as he was introduced. My
father heard about me in the news like most people.
He was surprisingly concerned. It was nice seeing
him again. I never thought that I'd ever see him
again. Guess it took me nearly dying for this
reunion to take place.

 Seeing my mother, I could have done

without but my father. That was almost a pleasant moment. However, seeing my father opened the flood gates in my mind to the abuse I suffered as a child. Memories about my uncle and what he did to me...about what happened the day I left. I just couldn't face it.

Once my dad left, Jaelyn was able to bring the kids into the room to see me. I was so excited to see them. The time that I got to spend with them helped keep my mind off of the past. I also wanted to provide my children something more than what my father gave me—his presence. I want to try to be more available to my children not only financially but physically as well. Who am I kidding? My children are probably better off without me.

Visiting hours were over. I decided to turn on the television to see what was going on in the world. Ironically, I was still the top story of the day. I was amused at the things they were saying about me, my life, and my past. This time people were asking question about me, figuring things out. The public was now realizing that what they saw of me in N'Step was not real. I was nowhere close to who I appeared to be.

Chapter 17
The Show Must Go On

"Today on Inside News, Multi-Award winning pop singer Tiffy Stone is at it again. Shown here by amateur video shopping. Her movements erratic and irrational at times. She was seen going throughout the shopping center, almost manic in her demeanor, snatching clothes off the rack and running throughout the stores looking dazed and confused.

Later in the day, the twenty-two-year-old singer was seen running out the store with her daughter two-year-old daughter Taylor, dragging her at times throughout the strip mall. Stone's behavior had become more bizarre since having her second child with heir to the oil empire Preston Fritzgerald."

After being released from the hospital, I snuck out quietly in the night. I stayed at a hotel until things died down. Christian had to go back home to Florida and suggested that I go back with him. He did not have to do much convincing. The house was on the beach, it was quiet. It was what I needed.

The first night there, was quiet. We sat out back to watch the waves and drinking some beer. Christian taking my hand and placing it on his lap. It was at that moment when I felt safe for the first time. I was secure. I was right where I was supposed to be. Christian loved that I was so close, so free with my affections. I have to admit, I loved it too.

Even though I did not know where Richard was, I did not care. In that moment I swore that I would not let him control my life anymore. Although I did not want to live in fear of what ifs, I could not shake the feeling that I needed to keep a watchful eye. I also wanted to try and be a good father to my children and become a better example for them. I needed to go visit Tiffy and make sure that she was taken care of and ensure that our daughter Taylor was okay.

I had not turned on the television since coming home with Christian. It did not take a rocket scientist to figure out that I was still the top news story. How could I not be? My whole life was now accessible to the media now that they knew who my family was. Surprisingly, the media nor the public cared about why I kept my life private, they just wanted dirt. Since my parents made their presence known as well as my sister everyone was now vying to get the story of my life. Fortunately, most of my family kept to themselves. However, my evil step brother Damon was another story. He was all too ready to make a statement.

Lies about me hiding my blackness were tossed about but soon discredited since I had never hidden the fact that my mother was black. Reason for my running away from a wealthy home life made for interesting talk. People were questioning why a boy from a privileged lifestyle would throw it all away to be with his adult boyfriend. It also came out that I may have had a hand in my uncles disappearance.

The public was forgiving of my homosexuality. They were even sympathetic to my abusive relationship and applauded my attempt to flee from it. However, once Tiffy Stone, America's sweetheart the ideal mate of ex band mate MJ had my child, the public began to view me as a villain. After hiding out with Christian for weeks, I decided to get away. While Christian went away on tour and promoted his charity organization, I went to visit Tiffy and our child.

I spent a few weeks at Tiffy's with my sweet little Taylor. She is definitely mine. Blonde hair, blue-green eyes, and olive skin. Both she and Tiffy were glad to see me. Tiffy and I continued to maintain our friendship even after she lost her love MJ because of me.

Time with her and our daughter was relaxing. I told Tiffy of my plans to disappear for awhile. She agreed that some time away from the media would be good for me. Tiffy and I were hanging out by the pool luxuriating, she suggested with her southern accent, "You know what I was thankin'? That we both should just go down to Texas and hang out with Jaelyn and the kids. Who's goin' to find us in Texas."

"That would actually be a good idea but what about your husband?" I smiled and flicked water in Tiffy's face.

"What about him? Let's just go. He and PJ can spend some time together."

Tiffy and I had always had a close bond; it was strange that she had no problems leaving her new husband and baby boy behind. But then again, I was no better.

The next day, I went to the mall and limping my way through for a bit of shopping therapy. My newly acquired body guard James, was not amused. A couple of times I would see him rolling his eyes as I stopped by the cosmetics counter checking out various products. After about an hour or so, we ended up at the electronics department at Sears. While walking through the electronics department I stopped dead in my tracks and gazed at the television screens. My worst nightmare being broadcast to the masses.

"Today on Inside News, our top story involves one of today's hottest international pop star—Elesin Vollan. Known for his flamboyant presence on stage, it is the twenty-two year-old's off stage life that has him once again in the midst of scandal.

"New images have hit the Internet showing a young Vollan engaged in various sex acts with two unidentified older men. Vollan's relationship with these men is unknown at this time, but it is certain that these images depict a deplorable act on a child.

The graphic photos were first revealed on Jacobsworld.com, which has had 523,500 hits in two days. Vollan's life before N'Step has been something of a well kept secret…

We will keep you updated with the latest developments as this story unfolds. Keep it here on Inside News for late-breaking celebrity news.

Next..."

"Fuck me!" I mumbled as I stood frozen in shock with my eyes focused on what seemed like a hundred big screen televisions broadcasting the most traumatizing time of my life. I thought to myself, *how could this have happened?* My heart was racing and my phone began ringing non-stop. I disregarded all calls but one—my publicist, Janet.

"Hello?"

"Have you seen the news?" she shouted into the receiver.

"Uh, yeah! I'm standing in the fuckin' electronics department of Sears. Every television is tuned to this shit." I was outraged at this new revelation of pictures from my past coming back to haunt me. The idea of having something presented to the public of a life that I had never quite come to terms with was frightening.

"Where did these images come from?"

"I don't know..." I replied, practically out of breath as I began running out of the store in a mad dash, hoping that no one would immediately recognize me. Panic consumed my body as I asked for advice on how to handle the situation. We had to assess the damage this could do to my already-tarnishing image. It was going to be hard to control the images of my abuse from the viewing public and even harder to erase them from the Internet.

The images being shown were unlike those that had appeared before. The snapshots of me in drag kissing men at clubs were never really a secret. I just like to keep my private life and my public life separate. After the initial media frenzy, they were chalked up to being in drunken fun or in the name of entertainment. The PR consultants and other staff members did a great job and had successfully downplayed the whole thing and kept my secret quiet.

The fact that I was a young man living with a boyfriend in L.A. somehow eluded the general public since I was married to the woman who was the mother of my son and who was raising my daughter. People naturally assumed that since she and I weren't living together that we were separated. That is, until my very public, very violent break-up with Richard.

Janet interrupted my thoughts, trying to be a voice of reason.

"I don't think anything can be done," she said. "The images...the videos...they're all over the Internet. Please, hun, do you know if there are any more?"

"Yes." I was getting more frazzled with every passing minute, biting my bottom lip nervously and I was beginning to taste blood.

"How do you want to handle the situation? I mean, obviously, you'll need to make a statement."

"I was afraid that you were going to say that." I sighed.

"Those pictures from the past you could just blow off. But, honey, no one can sugarcoat these latest photos flooding the Internet. You may need to just give the people what they want, let them know that you are human and vulnerable just like everyone else," she rambled on as my bodyguard and I searched frantically for an exit. "Elesin, it's time for you to let people in. Let them get to know the real you. The fact that you are openly bi-curious or gay never affected your image, so why should this?"

"Because I'm not sure that I know how to talk about this or would want to. I...I just can't! I mean, I was just fourteen when those fucking pictures were taken. How could they? I was just a child!" I hissed as we finally made our way out of the store and into the crowd of fans and paparazzi that suddenly surrounded me once outside. Multiple flashing camera lights blinded me and temporarily disoriented my every sense of direction. "I just want this to go away."

"Well, there's no way around it. The photos are out there and you have no choice but to confront this...this abuse. You'll get more sympathy from the public," she explained. "We can try to work on this together. In the mean time, get home and think about what I've said."

This could not have happened at a worse time. Last year was stressful enough. I had been in trouble with my management team for being late, missing gigs and causing conflict within the group. I was still getting over the whole ordeal with Richard and was still dealing with the ordeal that was still making headlines.

Things for this year were supposed to be better for me. The pseudo charmed life I had struggled to maintain in the public eye was beginning to crumble. Diane was right. I was going to have to force myself to share the most horrific time of my life. Unfortunately, I's have to figure out how to come to terms with the abuse first.

All I could think about was how that fucking tape got leaked. Actually, I already knew the how and the who. The only question on my mind now was how to handle this fucked up situation.

As we drove away from the mass chaos that engulfed us, all the memories of abuse—the torture I had suffered as a child…and the life I tried hard to forget—began to resurface. Thirty minutes later as we arrived at our destination. I made a decision. "I guess it's time to return Oprah's call."

"You know what? Just set it up, I'll do it." I finally gave into Diane's suggestion to do the Oprah show. On my way back to Tiffy's, I got a call from Christian.

"Hey baby. Are you okay?"

"No. Not really." I answered. "I'm trying to figure out what my next steps should be."

"What are you thinking?"

"I'm thinking that I may need to do an interview. Then disappear for awhile."

"Who were you thinking of interviewing with? You know it would have to be someone well respected. Someone with a huge following."

"Yeah, I know. I am going to work with my publicist on this but she did mention Oprah."

"Those are good choices." We continued on with our conversation about coming out with my story and giving the public what they want, an insight into my life and why I left. Even though I was not sure I wanted to discuss the abuse I suffered as a child, I could not live with the fear that someone would discover the whole truth. At least doing an interview would allow me to control how much information the public was exposed to.

Shocked by the revelation of my under aged sex tape. I immediately drove back over the Tiffy's house. When I got there, she had already seen the video off the Internet. Tiffy was horrified, she cried for me and held me like a mother holds her hurt child. I was mortified. How could Richard do this to me? What was the fucking point? The hordes of paparazzi began to grow outside her home. Our bags were already packed. The next thing to do was to get to the airport without anyone knowing.

The tickets were already purchased by Tiffy's assistant. The bags were checked. The nanny and the baby were at the airport waiting. Then it was time for us to leave. We had my bodyguard drive us to Barnes and Noble where we ducked off to the back exit and another car met us. Sneaking off to the airport and meeting up with the nanny and Taylor. We got far away from where anyone really cared and far away from the media circus as I could get.

Jaelyn was all too happy to pick us up from the airport. She and Lynnea both were especially excited to meet Tiffy for the first time.

"Oh my God. Aren't you just a tiny little thing?" Jaelyn exclaimed, grabbing the five-foot-three Tiffy in her arms.

"Nice to meet you, lady. How are you?" Tiffy giggled. Jaelyn introduced her to the children as we loaded up into the car. The drive to Jaelyn's house was quick considering she lived only ten miles from the airport.

It was nice seeing the girls chatting and having a great time with each other. We hung out by the pooling taking in the spring sun, splashing around. Both Lynnea and Jerrod were especially glad to see me. They were not letting me out of their sights or grips.

As the day wore on, we were lounging around talking about our lives. The children had a lot going on. After awhile, the children got bored with me and began to give Taylor all of the attention the rest of the day. The girls and I went out to the backyard to discuss how I was going to handle the images being shown on various websites that cater to illegal pornography.

Jaelyn provided us with a pitcher of frozen margarita. Like a good hostess, she served us then took her place across from me at the bistro styled table.

"How did this video get out?" Jaelyn asked.

"My father told me that he burned those videos. The only reasonable explanation is that Richard held on to some for insurance," I answered.

We sat there in silence as we drank our adult beverages. Jaelyn and Tiffy didn't know what to say after that. After awhile, Tiffy suggested that I give a public statement. I needed to somehow get across to Richard that he didn't bring me down. The rest of the night was uneventful. It was quiet, it was comfortable and it was going to be home for as long as it could be.

The next morning, I woke up to the sounds of children playing. Heading towards the noise, I was greeted with hugs from all around. Once in the kitchen, I found Jaelyn and Tiffy sitting at the table drinking coffee and watching the news.

"Good morning sunshine. You sleep well?" Jaelyn asked as she began pouring me a cup.

"I'm great. So what's new in the news?"

"Well, they've said that the images from the video were removed and anyone found to be in possession or linking child pornography would be prosecuted," Jaelyn explained.

"Yeah. At least the video and images are being contained," Tiffy interjected. "It could have been a lot worse. Also, you may need to talk to your step brother Damon. He is bashing you all over the news."

"Of course he would. I don't know what his problem is with me. I had never done anything to him. And he'd better shut it before I tell them what he had done to me in school," I said.

"What did he do?" Tiffy asked her eyes bulged with curiosity.

"Yeah, what?" Both women trying to get their fill of gossip. Wanting to know more about me and everything I had and was going through. I felt obligated to tell them everything since they were after all, the mothers of my children.

The tears welling up in their eyes as I told them the abuse I suffered at the hands of both my uncle and my brother. The shit that I went through and the hell I experienced at the hands of my uncle and his girlfriend. Even I could not hold back my tears. But it was a great relief to let everything out. To not have to hide my true self to those I care about. It was very reassuring.

"Why don't you share your experience with the world? I am sure that you are not the only one who had gone through this," Tiffy suggested.

"I don't want to be the poster child for sexual abuse. It was hard enough telling you guys. I just could not imagine telling everyone this. What would they think of me?"

"They would think that you were brave for surviving this," Tiffy consoled. "Your story could help so many who are struggling with this abuse. Let the world now that this is not just an issue that plagues little girls and young women but it affects boys and young men as well."

"Exactly. Let them see that you are not ashamed and that if you can make it out then anyone can," Jaelyn added. I was so afraid of what people would think of me. The girls had a great point. I was not the only one this had happened to. But I made it. I could help inspire others. Maybe it was time for me to let the public in and share my experience. Let them know I am human and make mistakes. Show them that my uncle and Richard did not break me.

Tiffy and I had managed to stay under the radar for three weeks. No one knew where we were. The news programs were all speculated on what happened to us and where we were hiding.

It wasn't too long after my hiatus from the world that Tiffy began working on her new image. Her album was going to be hot. The press was still buzzing with inquiries about where I was and every once in a while; I'd hear tales of Elesin sightings. I loved those.

"He was last seen at a Starbucks."

Or better yet, *"The elusive pop star had appeared..."* I just loved to see those news stories about my possible whereabouts. I always found it interesting how I was the most sought after star but no one was really looking for me. If they did care about me or my whereabouts all they had to do was find my children or Christian. I was never too far behind.

Tiffy was back home to work on her family life with her new family. While Christian was on his world tour, I was ready to sneak off to work on my solo career. I met with producer in New York to shop around for new sounds. During my down time, I hung out with Ra'mon who was making his rounds in the circuit for drag pageants at various night clubs.

Ra'mon invited me to one of his favorite spots Over the Rainbow. There was one go-go dancer who could not keep his eyes off of me. He was really hot. Tan bod, short cropped dark brown hair, hazel eyes and abs for days. I quickly scooped him up. Literally. At only five-foot-eleven, I towered over his five-foot-six frame. We sat in a booth close to the bar listening to top forty techno beats and watching the various entertainers.

"So, how long have you worked here?" I asked.

"Not long. A few months," he answered as he slinked and swayed with every word. "I needed money for school and this was the quickest way to get it."

"I bet. You're very attractive," I added.

"Thank you." He smiled as he sipped his apple martini, pinky extended.

We sat there with swarms of young men made their presence known to me. Entertaining us with stories and offering us drinks, drugs and sex. I guess that Claude was getting bored with the conversation and crawled over into my lap. Straddling me. Grabbing my hair with his hand, he leaned in for a kiss. My hands gripping his tight ass as he rose up and down. Rubbing his crotch against mine.

"How do you want me?" He asked. Taking his tongue alongside my neck. I smirked. "I know what you'd like."

Kissing his was way down my body. Making his way to under the table, he took my dick into his hands and began working me with his mouth. Flicking his tongue in ways I'd never imagined.

"Oh shit," I groaned.

"You like that baby?" He continued working my dick as a crowd of people began to watch. It was exciting. I just tried hard not come too quickly. I calmed myself so that I could enjoy Claude's lips more. Then suddenly, I found myself in the midst of a mini orgy. Okay, a major orgy.

Pulsating techno beats filling the air. Bodies of all shapes and sizes rubbed against each other. The experience was mind blowing. To feel wanted...to be loved by admirers was the greatest high one could ever experience. My head whirled with unbelievable pleasure. My boding trembled with a mind numbing surges of electricity. I so love

BENEATH THE SURFACE

New York.

The next few months were especially busy for me; I was attempting to co-parent my children, write songs in my spare time and had meetings with various record labels. Once I found my sound, I was ready to shop it around. I wanted to have more creative freedom. There were some ideas I had that I presented the label and surprisingly they were all for it. Glam rock here I come.

While working on my upcoming album, Christian was on the final leg of his tour. Every once in awhile, I would get to fly out an watch him perform and have dinner with him. It was nice getting to spend time with him and sharing my music with him.

Christian and I sat out on the balcony enjoying the moonlight and each other's company from his room at the Bellagio in Las Vegas.

"So, what time do you leave tomorrow?" Christian asked.

"My flight is at two."

"That doesn't leave us much time to spend with each other before I take off."

"How much time do we need?" I winked. I ran my fingers through his hair. Christian just smiled. I knew that sly grin all too well. That was my cue and he placed his hands under me and lifted me up. He carried me back into the room and placed me down gently. I began helping him out of his clothes, and I began to run my lips along his chest up to his neck. We fell onto the bed, he ripped off my shirt...then he dropped to his knees to remove my pants.

His full lips wrapped around my massive growth.

"Don't stop," I exhaled. His mouth feeling great on my cock. Sucking me off until I came. My head still buzzing in ecstasy. He laid on top of me, rubbing himself against me, kissing me deeply. My hands caressed his well defined chest and he took my dick into his hands and worked me until I let out a moan. He took his kissed down to my nipples and gave each one the attention they needed.

He lifted my legs up and eased his rock hard dick into my ass and if felt so good as we established our rhythm. I could barely stand it. He made love to me like no one ever had before. I thought that what Richard and I had was love but it wasn't until this moment that I realized that wasn't true. This is what I've been missing—the connection of our minds, our bodies...was unfathomed until now. I felt so light headed as my body shook uncontrollably with pleasure that I almost fainted. Then he came inside me, letting out a soft grunt, he rested his sweat body on top of mine and said, "Te amo, mi amor."

"Me too baby."

We slept peacefully in each other's arms. It was a great way to end the night.

I was meeting with my agent Diane; apparently big plans were in the works. Plans that not only involved my solo album but an interview to answer probing questions that had been plaguing the minds of the general public. The big interview was scheduled for the beginning of the year. If there were no setbacks, it would coincide with the release of my first album.

It had been nearly a year since I've been away from the spotlight. N'Step was finishing their tour off their third album when I began working on my solo project with Arista Records. My sound may have started in pop…but my body and soul were made for glam rock. I'm bringing glam back bitches in 1999.

I loved singing and writing songs but I knew that life after a boy band would be very difficult. No one has ever really found success as a solo artist after being in a boy band. Well, with the exception of Christian – it doesn't happen all too often. Maybe one could get lucky and strike a hit with one song. But I wanted to be more than a one hit wonder.

I had been working with some great producers who created a great sexy sound that fit me and the direction I wanted to go in. The rhythmical bass lines and the smooth rhythms going through one's body emanated to pure sex. My album was going to be a hit.

"This track right here is en fuego," JD said as we listened to our finished product. We collaborated with a few known people in the industry like MaDonna, Bowie and Queen.

"Thanks, I'm so excited," I cheered as I moved my body to the melodic sound.

"I think that this song will song here will be the shit. I can already hear it in the clubs," he gloated. We tweaked a few more songs and then it was off to market. Same game, different players.

We had three weeks to prepare for the show.

I had to rehearse with the dancers every day. My schedule this winter was pretty busy and chaotic. It was great. Jaelyn and the kids were in L.A. with me before I went off to tour. Lynnea who was growing up so fast in her nine years; thought it was cool to have a dad who sang and did videos. Jerrod who was now six just loved being around his dad.

"Daddy, can we come watch you at rehearsal today?" Lynnea asked.

"Sure. You can critique my performance."

"Cool!" she said as she jumped into my arms for a hug. Jaelyn was more interested in shopping and decided to pass on watching my practices. Besides, it gave her a nice break from the children. It was nice having the children around watching what I do. My son even got in on the action and tried some of the moves. Rehearsals were about three hours long. Afterwards, the children and I went out and met with their mother for dinner. There we chatted about my tour dates and locations.

Oprah booked me for an hour special with me to discuss everything that had gone on in my life. She is pretty awesome. I actually got to meet with her at her home for lunch with my Jaelyn and kids. We got to discuss ideas for the show and questions that were off limits.

I responded, "You can ask me anything and I'll answer as best that I can."

Well, she was quiet enthusiastic about that. We spoke on the phone for awhile as I gave her some insight into my childhood and the abuse I had suffered. She was very easy to talk to and made me feel very comfortable. Hopefully, she would not throw me a curve ball and make me cry or have a surprise guest.

I was to perform on the American Music Awards show January 19th; two week after my CD came out. Pre-sales of my album were breaking records. After the buildup of my new album, and the interview with Oprah, everyone was waiting in anticipation of what was to come. Would I be a flop? Would I live up to everyone's expectations?

I had never been so nervous in my life even with my family, friends and Christian waiting and watching with anticipation for me to close out the show. I was dressed head to toe in Prada. I rocked a pair of dark black stretch pants, a fitted button down black satin shirt with a charcoal gator printed corset.

As I stood in the dark on stage, I awaited my cue. The lights hit and I was on. People rose to their feet as danced to the hypnotic pulsating beats. I made sure to hit every mark, and strutted my stuff across the stage. The crowd screaming with approval and by the end of the performance-- everyone was on their feet. Clapping with enthusiasm and support. I did it. I really did it.

Working the American Music Awards in to promote my new song of my album was such a high and people were still raving about it. My album was climbing up the charts and had settled into the number two spot, damn that Brandy. I had booked five live spots on various day and night time television shows to perform my song. Then I would begin my countdown until my Oprah appearance.

As January 29th was drew near and I

beginning to get cold feet. The anxiety had been building up so much that I almost canceled. Jaelyn had reassured me that nothing to worry about, she and the kids were going to stand by me every step of the way. I wanted to spend time with my family and friends to prepare them for what they were going to hear.

I had a well deserved break from all the madness to prepare for my interview. Everyone had been buzzing about the upcoming television event. Oprah herself advertised that the show would be, "The most revealing look at a rising new solo artist." Oh the pressure.

The most talked about show was about to debut signaling the end of the season. The nerves were getting the best of me. Christian and Jaelyn were both waiting nervously with me in "green room" as the minutes ticked down to show time. To get my mind off of my pending interview, we chatted about the reasons for the room being called a green room, especially since neither the room nor anything in it was actually green.

I was so anxious that I fidgeted fiend-like making Christian just as nervous as he sat waiting for me to go on.

"Sientete! Por Favor..." Christian grumbled and he grabbed my arm to stop me from pacing the green room. Jaelyn smiled and shook her head. She'd seen me in every emotional state but she had never seen me a nervous wreck.

"Sorry, I'm just a little bit nervous," I said as I checked out the various pictures that adorned the coffee colored walls. "Do you think that this was a mistake?" I asked as I sat down next to Christian with my hands covering my face in shame.

"Baby, you don't have anything to worry about besides, we'll be here the whole time," he comforted. I leaned over to rest my head onto his left shoulder. He kissed the top of my head and continued to say, "Just know that I'm proud of you for having the fucking balls to speak out and share part of your life. You've been quiet for too long, no more secrets." I looked up into Christian's gorgeous brown eyes and I finally felt calm.

People were starting to flood back into the room to get me ready for my appearance. I wanted to be more natural, so I left the liner at home and my hair was almost back to its natural golden blonde state. Hair and makeup personnel were frantically ensuring that I was television ready, to let the public see me for who I really was...no more smoke and mirrors.

"Elesin Vollan was first introduced to the world when he joined the pop group N'Step. Once in the band, it was apparent that he was the breakout star of the group. With his rock star attitude and his model good looks, it was pretty hard not to notice.

This twenty-two-year-old heart throb has transfixed us with not only his amazing singing voice but his antics off stage as well. As Elesin's career continued to skyrocket, the more secrets of his personal life began to emerge. Everything from the sexual abuse he's suffered as a child to his various sexual encounters with men quickly overshadowed the talents of the band.

Over the course of his life in and out of N'Step, Elesin has faced many life changing obstacles that not only affected his role within the group but his personal life. Here today to share some insight into his life…Elesin Vollan!" She yelled. I walked onto the set with long quick strides into her open arms. She whispered into my ear, "You ready for this?"

"No, but I'm here." We laughed as I proceeded to give a wave to the applauding audience and take my seat onto the tangerine orange chair.

Oprah shook her head, "Elesin, Elesin, Elesin--"

"I know." I chuckled. Oprah gave me a look as if I were in some sort of trouble.
She went on to ask, "Where do I even begin with you?"

"Anywhere you like. I'm ready." I replied as I rubbed my hands across my thighs bracing myself for the arsenal of questions.

"Okay. We'll start from the beginning. You were one of five hot young men from the singing group N'Step. You were quickly singled out and labeled the bad boy of the group. Everything you did good and bad, mostly bad was picked up by every electronic and paper media outlet. Yet even though everything from your wild parties, hook ups and break ups were documented, we really knew nothing about you. How were you able to that, keep your life a secret?"

I chuckled, "Yeah, I know. It still shocks me that with all my celebrity, no one even cared enough to ask me fundamental questions like, who I was or where I came from? My best guess is that no one cared to ask me."

"But in a way, was it your plan or the management teams plan to keep your background shrouded in secrecy. Everything from where you were born, your age, and even your sexuality, was it all deliberate?

I shifted a bit in my seat, crossing my left leg over the right. I turned my body slightly away from her as he posed the question. My mind whirling with ways to answer the question without being too vague or sketchy.

"In the beginning it was deliberate as far as my sexuality goes but when it came to my race, background or whatever, if I were asked the question then I'd answer...Truthfully. My sexuality was something I had always been open about in my circle of friends. But it was agreed between the management team and me to keep that on the back burner.

"At any point did that change? Did you want to go public with that part of your life in regards to your sexuality?" She asked.

"Yes. After being in the group for over a year – it was just too stressful to keep that part of my life, my sexuality hidden. Then once the pictures came out, some part of me was relieved.

"Relieved that you no longer had to keep that secret anymore?"

I nodded, "Yes. But the management team covered and made it all seem as if it were in drunkin' fun or just – who knows what. It was hard for awhile trying to keep my identity. My true self."

She continued to ask me where I was originally from then went into who my parents were. I answered each question, shifting my gaze from the Oprah then to the audience members. After about fifteen minutes of basic Q & A's, she when into the hard core questions. I planted my feet firmly onto the floor, with my hands on my thighs.

"Did all the behavioral issues or our acting out, stem from any sort of abuse?" She asked as she leaned into me.

I took a deep breath before answering, "Yes."

"Sexual abuse?"

"Yes, unfortunately." I began to tear up a bit one she touch on the abuse that suffered as a child. She was kind enough to got into a break for I completely fell apart.

"Are you okay, Elesin?" She asked as she placed her hand on top of my hand. I nodded as I dabbed my eyes with the tissue that she offered. Once I collected myself, her makeup person retouched our faces – and we were back on.

She questioned me about me being able to maintain a smile through the pain. I informed her that, "it was just something I grew accustomed to doing my whole life. Putting on a front so that people would never discover that I was in pain. I had to keep friends at a distance trying to hide the truth of my abuses."

Oprah continued on with her line of questions that outlined the course of my life before and after being discovered.

"Okay. Fast forward to when you began your singing career. How did you get discovered?"

"I had been modeling for awhile. In between my jobs, one of my good friends, Christian, had given me the opportunity to singing with him on his background vocals. Eventually, someone had gotten a hold of my demo tapes and my agent set me up with the producer of Intercontinental Records, Neal Diamond. The rest is history." Oprah's eyes lit up as her interviewer's hard luck story began to take on a more positive spin. Then she took a deep breath and went into the relationship I had with Richard and the events that led up to my attack.

"Let's discuss the events that occurred after the attack; those images and the video of you being raped. What were your thoughts when you found out that the video was making its debut on the Internet?"

"Honestly, my first thought was oh shit." I laughed along with the audience members who were riveted by my story.

"How did you handle it?" She leaned back into her chair with her hands resting on her lap.

"After the shock of learning that my abuse was broadcast—It's hard to explain, but it was like I was being raped all over again. I actually went home and cried."

She followed up by asking, "Do you know who put the video and those images out there?"

"If I were to guess, I'd say Richard. After all, who else would want to humiliate me like that?"

"When did your relationship with Richard change? When did the abuse start?" She asked.

"I guess it started pretty early on, I met some people at various clubs, got exposed to a different lifestyle and his was jealous, probably for good reason. But it got really bad when I started N'Step."

"Are you saying that he had reason to abuse you?"

"That did sound bad. I mean, I did cheat and had some overlapping relationships and I think that was the trigger. In no way do I believe that there is any reason for physical abuse, I'm just saying that, I pressed a lot of buttons."

She looked at her cards to ensure that she was on track with her line of questioning. The she asked, "At any point did you say, enough is enough and try to leave?"

"Yes."

"What happened with that?"

I winced as the internal debate within my mind to tell or not to tell. Finally, I gave in and decided to share that time in my life.

"It was just before I started touring with N'Step. He was so angry." I took a deep breath remembering that moment. "It was the first time that I felt that I was like, F you man, I am not dealing with this anymore and I bolted out the door. I went over to a friend's house all battered and bruised."

I relived my weak attempts to leave him as the events flashed in my mind. I shook my head remembering the threats he made against me and my children. I almost didn't hear the next question she asked.

"But you went back to him, why?"

"Well, when you are in a band, it's kind of hard to hide. He would turn up at public events and win me back."

She leaned into me and asked, "After everything that Richard has done, the assault, the publication of your pictures and videos of abuse— do you still love him?"

The lump in my throat grew, nearly closing up my airway that I opened my mouth slightly before answering. I was caught of guard and embarrassed at the realization that deep down inside, I still had feelings for that man. Strong feelings that I thought had all been resolved.

Oprah noticed the shock on my face from my internal struggle and places her hand upon mine which rested on the arm of the chair.

I laughed uncomfortably as the audience gasped when I answered a hesitant, "yes." After that, I could hardly look her in her eyes. I could not believe that after all that work to rid myself of Richard, all the work to get my solo career off the ground, hell, I even kicked my coke habit—that I could not rid that man out of my heart.

She and the members of the audience listened intensely as I explained the situation and how I overcame that situation. Before I knew it the interview was over as Oprah ended by saying, "Wow! It was so great finally getting to talk with you and you sharing your story with us. I could talk to you all day. Up next, Elesin will be performing his hit song, Don't Care."

Four Letter Words

Four letter words. I love fours letter words. But of all the four letter words, why is hate the easiest to feel? Someone cuts us off-- BAM! Rage! Hate! Fuck! These four letter words seem to hit us hard. Love another four letter word that comes over us slowly and then finally BAM!

Overwhelming us into submission. You're in love. Spreading over you like a cancer; eating away at your body and soul. Four letter words; there is nothing in the world like them. Back to the bad four letter word Fuck. What is fuck? How is this word different than the other four letter words? How is it different than making love, the other four letter word? Let's evaluate this shall we? Love-making. . . Is full of passion once you in love it's hard to get out of it. It begins with tender kisses; all over your body. You love every inch of that person's body. Love making is something shared with a couple. . . (maybe trio) that is full of passion full of romance. Full of Love! That cute little four letter word.

Then there's the dirty little four letter

word. Fuck! This is something that can make you or break you. When it comes to Fucking; passion has nothing to do with it. Like Trent Reznor says, "I want to fuck you like an animal I want to feel you from the inside." It's all about that animal inside of all of us that you can't get from Love. That's why the lack of a good fucking can break you; especially if you are in a relationship.

Men all want women who are good enough to take to their mothers as well as to not be embarrassed to show off to their buddies. However, men also want or need that freak in the bedroom. The problem with that is that men usually don't know how to approach new ideas or fantasies with their women. They don't want their "innocent" wives or girlfriends to turn them down and close off all contact or possibilities. On the other hand, wives or girlfriends are too afraid to tell their man to: "Shove it up my ass!" "Harder!" "Faster!" Women don't want their good girl image to be tarnished leaving both parties frustrated and seeking that great "Fuck" elsewhere.

Love and Fuck? Two very distinct four letter words with such great meaning. Both words affect us in very different ways. Love is something that everyone want to be in. Fuck is something you wish to have. That's why you can get the fuck of your life with a stranger better than with your partner. There are no inhibitions. When one goes after that great fuck there is a commonality between each person. Letting go and being free--Free to do other four letter words like: Plow, slam, bite, grab, slap, lick, suck and well, you get the point. . . What do you get with love? You get held and lots of hugs. . .

Secret Lover

No longer can I bare you at a distance.
No longer can I stand the quick glances.
No one knows who you are,
Or that you're the one that makes me smile.
Secret lover.

You are my heart and soul.
I want the whole world to know.
I don't want to be afraid,
Of this love that we both share.
Secret Lover.

I love how you make me feel.
My body shivers when you're near.
I know our love is for real.
I just can't let you go.
I want the whole world to know.

I need you to know,
That I'll never let you go.
I want you by my side.
Holding me tight; loving me.
You're my secret lover.